His name is

PATRICK DAWLISH

He is a very large man, with vast shoulders
that his well-cut suit cannot conceal. But for
the broken nose, a legacy of an early battle
in the boxing ring, he would be as
handsome as he is massive . . .
He is always jumping in with both feet
where the police fear to tread. And no thief,
blackmailer or murderer ever comes up
against a tougher, more resourceful,
deadlier enemy than

PATRICK DAWLISH

A NEST OF TRAITORS, one of the
Patrick Dawlish series, is by John Creasey
writing as Gordon Ashe, of which there are
now over forty titles and many have been
published by Corgi Books.
Born in 1908, John Creasey has married
three times, has three sons and has homes in
both Wiltshire, Great Britain and in
Arizona, USA, where his books sell more
than in any other country. Overall, John
Creasey's books have sold nearly a hundred
million copies and have been translated into
28 languages.
As well as an extensive traveller, he has a
particular interest in politics and is the
founder of *All Party Alliance*, which
advocates a new system of government by
the best candidates from all parties and
independents. He has fought in five
parliamentary by-elections for the
movement.

John Creasey
as Gordon Ashe

A Nest of Traitors

CORGI BOOKS
A DIVISION OF TRANSWORLD PUBLISHERS LTD
A NATIONAL GENERAL COMPANY

A NEST OF TRAITORS

A CORGI BOOK 0 552 09162 6

Originally published in Great Britain
by John Long Limited

PRINTING HISTORY

John Long edition published 1970
Corgi edition published 1973

This book is set in Baskerville 9/10 pt.

Corgi Books are published in Transworld Publishers, Ltd.,
Cavendish House, 57–59 Uxbridge Road, Ealing,
London, W.5.

Made and printed in Great Britain by
Richard Clay (The Chaucer Press), Ltd., Bungay, Suffolk.

**NOTE: The Australian price appearing on the
back cover is the recommended retail price.**

CONTENTS

CHAPTER ONE

THE VISITOR

The child lay sleeping.

Her hair, dark and long, fell half over her pale face, half over the pillow. She breathed evenly and softly. A woolly animal lay near, her hand clutching its fur, as if even in sleep she sought its comfort. The morning light spread about the small room, touching the pretty bed, the fragile chairs. A large wicker hamper stood beneath the window, lid thrown back, little dolls and big dolls, toy animals of all sizes and kinds, tumbled there. A ladder with Snow White and the Seven Dwarfs clinging to it was draped over one side, Noddy at the foot looking as if ready and eager to jump down on to the pale pink carpet.

In the next room, a man snored—not heavily, not loudly, but rhythmically. For a long time it had been the only sound.

Soon, there was another: a sharp click which seemed very loud. But the child did not stir and the snoring did not change. The intrusive sound was not repeated, but soon there was another: a creak on the stairs. This was repeated several times, but neither of the sleepers stirred.

The door of the room where the child slept was open a few inches, and the room where the man slept alone was just across a narrow landing. A faint shadow appeared at the child's doorway, and gradually the door began to open. As it did so, something swayed from the top of the door and swung gently across the opening, making a faint whirring sound: there was a stifled gasp. But still the child and the man slept undisturbed.

On the landing outside the child's door stood a man who had no right there. He was short and very broad-shouldered, young, black-haired. He swayed back as the object swung, until he saw what it was: a toy 'man', dangling at the end of a parachute which was fixed to the lintel above the door frame, as if to protect the child. It was very life-like, but now made

7

no sound at all. The man kept a hand on the door and glanced into the room. He stared intently at the child for a few moments. Up till then he had been expressionless, his face hard; now, it relaxed into a smile.

He drew the door to where it had been, and crossed the landing. The snoring was now fitful, as if the sleeper had turned. That door was ajar, too, wider open than the child's. There was no need for the intruder to push it wider still. He went in, sideways, all traces of the smile gone. When he was right inside the room, he was within five or six feet of the sleeping man, who lay facing the door.

The intruder's face changed; there was a kind of ruthlessness about him and he lowered his right hand to his coat pocket as he stepped closer to the sleeper. This man was big. He was sprawled right across a wide bed. One arm and hand, pyjama jacket sleeve pushed up nearly to the elbow, lay limp outside the bedclothes.

Once or twice he gave a little twitching movement, but nothing suggested he was on the point of waking.

The intruder took another step towards him, drawing a knife out of his pocket—a knife with a short, wide blade which brought a flash of brightness to the room, caught from the light of an open window. The blade of the knife pointed towards the sleeping man. The other held it easily between long, agile fingers.

He stopped a foot from the bed, looking down.

He stood there for what seemed a long time, changing his hold on the knife. The man in the bed moved again, and his head dropped into a different position, exposing his neck above the striped pyjamas.

Somewhere not far off, a church clock struck ... three, four, five, six.

A car engine sounded, distant at first, then louder; it passed the house and the sleeping man stirred again. In the street, a door slammed. This seemed the cue to the man with the knife, who moved forward and made one deliberate, murdering slash.

'Daddy,' the child called.
There was no answer.
'Daddy!' she called again, and still there was no answer.
She lay back on her pillow, looking at the window, frowning

8

with all the intensity of a child of eight. A sparrow fluttered close, seeming to peer in at her. She stayed motionless, hardly breathing, until a car moving in the street startled the bird and sent it flying off. The child pushed back the bedclothes and tiptoed across the floor to the window; she was tall enough to see out without rising on her toes. A dozen birds, sparrows and thrushes, speckled the lawn in front of this small, detached house, pecking at seed which her father had sown on some bare patches in the grass only the previous night.

She looked out on to a familiar sight to her and what would be a pleasant sight to most. This was in suburban north-west London, and was about twenty years old, so that the modern style houses stood in comfortably large gardens, each a little different from its neighbour. Most were white, the roofs of red, brown, green or blue tiles. The gardens were of various shapes, each with a lawn and many, on this day in June, showing roses, antirrhinums, asters, also some late, vari-coloured tulips. There were flowering shrubs, a few mature trees, even vegetables, all enclosed within trim, well-tended hedges.

They called this place the Hallows End Garden Suburb. The postman, pushing a bicycle, turned into the street at one end, and, some distance away, a white-capped, grey-smocked milkman walked up a path carrying his bottle-filled wire basket. Nearly opposite, a young and very pretty girl, a sack slung over her back, was easing a newspaper into a letter box.

The child tired of watching the scene and the birds, and turned to the door.

'Daddy,' she said in a pensive voice.

He had told her that it was good to be able to stay on her own, without being frightened, and had orders never to wake him unless she was frightened—and there was nothing to frighten her on this lovely sunlit morning. But suddenly she reached the door, and saw that the parachute and parachutist had fallen from the thin nail in the lintel.

'Oh!' she gasped in a muted tone of distress, and dropped down to her knees.

First she picked up the parachutist, a finger-sized plastic figure, beautifully proportioned and 'real' looking. She straightened a bent arm and a bent knee and soothed and patted him, straightened his harness and readjusted the parachute, which opened automatically as the figure slid down the string.

Then she looked up.

She could not reach the nail in the lintel on which her father hung the parachute every night, and she had never wanted to reach it so much. She glanced across at the door of her father's room, surprised that it was closed. For it was *never* closed; that was a bargain her father had made with her when she had come to stay with him.

'There's no need to be frightened, Kathy, if the doors are open.'

'I suppose there isn't,' she had agreed, dubiously.

'You'll be able to hear me downstairs—hear the radio and television,' he had reassured her. 'And if I have to be out at night I'll make sure someone else is here. Do you understand? I'll never leave you alone.'

And he had kept his word.

She could not possibly dream of the difficulties this had caused him; nor how often, since his wife's—her mother's—death, the loneliness of the house had driven him nearly mad. At times he would have given anything to get up, switch off the television and go out—to a pub, to a movie, to his club, even to walk and walk until the pain of remembering eased. But he had never let the child down and never before had she found the door shut.

Had the wind closed it?

She went halfway across the landing, then turned and scurried back for her slippers. *Never walk about without slippers on, Kathy.* And she never did, except when she forgot. As she pushed her toes into the slippers, she thought: I expect he didn't hear me because the door was shut.

She skipped across the landing again, happy and confident; he wouldn't mind her going in as the door was shut.

She turned the handle and pushed—but the door didn't open. Her face fell in disappointment as she tried again, but could not get the door to move. In a sharp, scared voice, she called:

'Daddy!'

He did not answer.

She pushed and turned the handle, but the door remained shut. There was no key in the lock; no way she could open it.

'Daddy!' she cried, in sudden, overwhelming panic. 'Daddy, the door's locked! Let me in!'

But there was no sound, no response at all when she began to bang on the door and push, and calling 'Daddy, Daddy, Daddy!' in a voice which was breaking as if she were near tears.

At last she gave up and went back to the warm familiarity of her own bedroom. She climbed on to the bed and picked up the toy, half-dog, half-rabbit, and put her thumb to her lips. Although nearly nine, she often soothed herself this way. She lay on her side, comforted but still very uneasy. She simply did not understand. She *couldn't* understand. But soon, she began to think. He would wake up and open the door soon, she was sure he would. It must be very early. But it wasn't so early, or the postman and the paper girl would not have been in the street. It must be nearly eight o'clock, and she had to leave for school before half-past.

The church clock began to strike. '... six ... seven ... eight.' There, it was eight o'clock!

She sprang off the bed and went rushing across the landing again, half screaming: 'Daddy, wake up, it's time for school!' But nothing she did won any response.

There was a vivid change in her, now; obviously she was nearly panic stricken. Her face was tense and pale and her eyes abnormally bright. She knew that she had to do something. Her thoughts veered, from getting into trouble if one were late for school, to wondering what had happened to Daddy. She would have to telephone somebody. She *must* telephone somebody, but—who? She didn't know any number except the number of this house. Her father had made her learn it off by heart, in case, when out of the immediate neighbourhood, she should get lost.

'Go to a policeman,' he had said, 'and give him the number of the house, the name of the street and the telephone number.' It had been ages before she had got them right. *'My name is Kathy Kemball, I live at Number 17 Hogarth Avenue, Hallows End Garden Suburb, Hallow 3456.'* Such an easy number, her father had said, half scolding, half laughing at her. And now it was vivid in her mind.

'Go to a policeman.'

That's what she must do—find a policeman!

She hurried back to her room, and began to dress. It was not, she decided, necessary either to clean her teeth, or brush her hair. Dressed at last she went to the head of the stairs, and

11

hesitated.

'Oh Daddy!' she cried wildly, and rushed back to the closed door. But it was no use, there was no answer, and she couldn't open it. She went down the stairs, half-sobbing, to the front door where two letters and a newspaper were on the mat. She picked these up and put them on a little table, then opened the door.

The sunlight shone brightly across the garden. She hesitated, then with another flare of panic realised that the door might close on her, and she hadn't a key. She pushed the door catch back and secured it so that she could not lock herself out, then walked along the crazy-paving path towards the street.

'Frank,' the woman from the next door house said at the same moment, 'that poor child's going off to school very early.'

'That poor child,' echoed her husband, 'has probably had a better breakfast than I have!'

'No, I'm serious,' his wife insisted. She was grey-haired, sixty-ish faded of feature, her expression one which suggested that she was constantly on the threshold of frustration. Her husband looked ten or fifteen years her junior, dark-haired, tall, lean, big-boned and without an ounce, not even a hint, of flabbiness about him. He looked idly out of the window. 'She's going like the wind.'

'Which you can hardly say of yourself this morning.'

'Frank——'

'Oh, stop worrying!' exclaimed her husband. 'She isn't the only motherless child in the world, and her father doesn't neglect her, that's for sure.'

He looked resignedly at his wife, still staring along Hogarth Avenue. Theirs was a single storey house and their kitchen faced the northern end of the estate. A series of coincidences enabled them to see almost the full length of the road, although houses and fences, trees and walls, shrubs and trim hedges obscured the view from most windows.

'You're as bad as——'

'Frank, she hasn't done her hair, and she's usually so well-groomed—and look, she hasn't got her school satchel! There's something wrong. I sensed it the moment I saw her. I'm going after that child.'

'Not in your dressing-gown and knitted slippers,' he scoffed.

'Oh drat it!' his wife cried, and then she faced him squarely, looking quite massive and commanding. '*You'll* have to go, you're dressed. Hurry! If she gets into the main road...'

The husband began to protest, but something in his wife's manner, as well as a sudden sliver of fear in his own mind, stopped him. The man Kemball never let the child start out for school on her own, and always saw to it that neighbours with children brought her back.

'Do hurry, Frank,' his wife urged, as she followed him to the back door.

She watched him striding along, out of the gateway, towards the High Street and the busy main road, noting that several other neighbours were going the same way. She began to wonder what, if anything, could have happened, and whether the child was as scared as she, Madge Halkin, had thought. She had always had a soft spot for Kathy. To lose one's mother at the age of seven was a terrible thing. Kemball ought to get married again, not simply have a night or two out on the tiles most weeks, he'd been widowed long enough, and that child needed a mother's care.

'That child' stood at the corner, looking up and down, hardly aware of the thick, fast moving traffic, looking desperately for a policeman. But there was none in sight.

CHAPTER TWO

THE POLICEMAN

The Deputy Assistant Commissioner of the Metropolitan Police, Mr. Patrick Dawlish, was up early that morning, for he had an important conference with the Commissioner and all the A.C.s, Commanders and Deputy Commanders—the V.I.P.s of New Scotland Yard. He was not enthusiastic about the forthcoming meeting but he had no choice, unless by happy chance some urgent call came, in which case he would bid the gentlemen who investigated London's crime 'good morning', and apply himself to the subject which interested, in fact, absorbed him. His wife sometimes said it obsessed him. This subject might loosely be called international crime, or crime which had international significance. Dawlish, a tall, broad, fair-headed man, was only just saved by a broken nose from being spectacularly handsome. He had acquired his interest in foreign problems during the Second World War. At that time very young, he had been parachuted behind the enemy lines so many times that he claimed to have lost count after the first dozen.

'If you can survive twelve,' he had said, 'for all you know your luck might be in for ever. Certainly for the duration.'

His 'luck', if that was the right word, had certainly been in. There had been other contributory factors, of course. His own cool, calculating courage for instance; his skill in planning every drop, in fact everything he did, with extreme care; his reflexes and his physical fitness—he was, all these years later, a remarkably fit man—and his sense of timing. Added to all this, he had an almost incredible ability to win friends quickly as well as a useful knowledge of the German language. There was the probably apocryphal story of the time when he had dropped among a German paratroop company, setting them all roaring with laughter at the story he told, of how he had fooled the stupid English!

After the war this giant of a man had not been content to settle down to fruit-farming and pig-keeping, although he had tried. It had taken a very short time for Felicity, his wife, to realise and acknowledge that he was living only half-a-life. She had soon given up protesting when, hypnotised by some problem involving crime and violence, he had so eagerly 'lent a hand'. Lending a hand had sometimes brought him into conflict with the police, and as often found him working with them. Then the day had come when poetic justice had been done and, presumably on the principle 'if you can't beat 'em, join 'em' he had been invited to join the Metropolitan Police as the Deputy Assistant Commissioner for Crime dealing with its international aspects,

'That will quieten him down,' the knowing ones had rejoiced.

At home, it had. Indeed he was the soul of correctitude in London. But overseas he remained the Patrick Dawlish who was prepared to take on all comers, break all laws in the pursuit of justice, and spread the legend that only those who knew him really believed.

This particular morning he had to prepare some reports

about the activities of the Mafia both in London, and throughout Europe. He had also to telephone a member of the Sûreté Nationale in Paris about a case of counterfeiting, and send several cables to Commonwealth countries regarding some ingenious passport frauds. All of these things must be done before the conference, which would begin at ten o'clock, so he was on his way to the office at the 'old Scotland Yard', from which he operated. He walked. Behind him was a tall office building, at the top of which was his pent-house. Ahead were the Houses of Parliament, recently cleaned and looking unbelievably beautiful in the pale sunlight. He had a moment or two of regret for the Britain that used to be, then looked across the river at Lambeth Palace and spared a glance for Westminster Abbey. Two or three policemen saluted him, and he was crisp with his 'good morning'. As he strode across Parliament Square, and turned into Whitehall, Big Ben struck eight. So he had nearly two hours, and should get everything done.

He expected to be alone in his office, but his chief assistant, Childs, was there. Childs was a middle-aged man, a little careworn, often woe-begone, who looked older than his years. He had a remarkable knowledge of international law, of the laws of different countries, and also of policemen and criminals. Dawlish was gradually compiling a record of these and his own knowledge was extensive; but compared with Childs's, it was negligible.

'Good morning, sir,' Childs said.

' 'Morning. Have we run into any special problem?' asked Dawlish.

'No. I knew how much you wanted to get done before ten o'clock,' said Childs. 'Shall I make a start on the passport fraud report?'

'Do that,' agreed Dawlish, happily.

Childs disappeared into his own office, and Dawlish settled down in his. The office explained why he was still in the old building. It was a highly modernised, computerised department, on one side of which was a drawing bench, sloping down from the wall. On this were two world maps, in relief, dotted so that different colours showed. These helped Dawlish locate people they were calling or who were calling them. He could make instant contact with any police force in the world. The maps were divided in such a way that the time zones were immediately identifiable: he could tell at a glance what the local time was, at any given British Standard Time, anywhere in the world. Relieved that Childs had taken over one of the more routine chores, he was immersed in the Mafia problem, and becoming more and more appalled by its ramifications, when the telephone buzzed and a light glowed on one of his telephones. This was his direct line to the main Criminal Investigation Department, which was housed in the new building, off Victoria Street. This telephone was seldom used, and whenever it was, carried a sense of urgency.

He lifted the receiver.

'Patrick Dawlish.'

'Good morning, sir.' This was a Superintendent Lancaster, one of the old school of Yard men, and liaison between Dawlish's branch and the usual C.I.D. business, which so often overlapped. 'Lancaster here, I think something has turned up that you should know about.'

'Yes.' Dawlish prompted him.

'You remember Kemball, sir. David Kemball?'

'I certainly do,' said Dawlish.

'He's dead, sir. Been murdered.' While Dawlish reacted to the shock of this, Lancaster went on: 'In particularly harrowing circumstances, too.'

'Oh,' Dawlish said heavily. 'What circumstances?'

'A neighbour found his child wandering in the streets, looking for a policeman. Kemball had told her always to look for a policeman if she was lost or in trouble. The trouble this morning was that her father had locked his door, which he never did normally, and she could not wake him by calling. The neighbour found two of our men from the Hallows End Sub-Division, and they had the good sense to leave the child with the neighbour while they broke down the door.'

Lancaster paused, as he often did, for effect. Dawlish spoke into the pause:

'Didn't Kemball lose his wife?'

'A little over a year ago in a car accident.'

'And he didn't remarry?'

'I gather not, Mr. Dawlish. They found ...' this time Lancaster's tone held a note of reproof, he did not want his climax spoiled '... they found Kemball in bed with his throat cut. He'd been dead only two or three hours.'

Dawlish had a mental vision: of the child banging on the

16

father's door, and crying out his name.

'Good thing about those neighbours,' he remarked gruffly. 'Anything missing?'

'No, sir, not as far as we know, though the whole house had been ransacked. The only room not turned inside out was the little girl's. A lot of quite valuable things were left untouched, most of it easy enough to move. You may remember Kemball collected miniatures and china.'

'Yes, I do.'

'It's all there. And there were sixty odd pounds in his wallet, sir, which was left open on a chair by the bedside.'

'Odd.'

'I don't understand you, sir.'

'To kill first and search after,' Dawlish explained.

'Do you regard that as odd?' asked Lancaster sceptically. 'It seems very normal to me. To make quite sure that he couldn't be disturbed and then ...' Lancaster caught his breath. 'I see what you mean, sir. He had gone to find something and he didn't know where it was, so you'd expect him to keep Kemball alive long enough to tell him.'

'That's it, precisely,' Dawlish said. 'No more than odd, though, not necessarily significant. A really good professional search, you say.'

'Very thorough indeed, sir.'

'No prints, of course.'

'Nothing but Kemball's, the child's and a daily woman's, who comes afternoons and evenings, I understand.'

'What time did you find out about this?' asked Dawlish.

'Just after eight, sir.'

'Someone's been very quick,' Dawlish remarked. He glanced at his watch. It was now only nine fifteen. He had an almost irresistible impulse to say he would go to the scene of action immediately, but at this time of the morning it would take at least an hour to get there; he couldn't get back, even if he spent only a little time at the scene, until mid-day! by then, with luck, the conference would be practically over.

'I'd like to get out there this afternoon,' he said.

'I'll tell Division to expect you, sir.'

'Thanks. Anything else at all, Superintendent?'

'Not really,' said Lancaster. 'I did wonder ...' he broke off.

'Go on.'

'I did wonder whether Kemball had been doing anything

17

you knew about.'

'No,' answered Dawlish. 'Not since the Boscowen job. But that doesn't mean he hasn't been very active.'

'Bound to have been,' said Lancaster. 'I hope we'll know a lot more before you get there.'

'I'll call you before I leave.' Dawlish rang off and sat back, frowning. He wasn't going to be able to concentrate on this new situation and finish the Mafia report, although that report was urgent. But—David Kemball, murdered. A man who had once been of inestimable help to Dawlish and the international organisation known, colloquially, as the Crime Haters. Kemball had hated crime with the same passionate intensity as Dawlish. There had even been a possibility that he would join the organisation in some capacity or other, but it would have taken Kemball out of England for much of the time, and he had not wanted to leave his wife alone so often. Dawlish had never met her but had the impression that Kemball's marriage had been one of those comparatively rare ones: near perfect.

That child . . .

'*Mafia*,' Dawlish said aloud, and straightened up in front of his desk. He had the kind of mind that could switch from one subject to another with no slackening in concentration, dealing with the new and more urgent task exclusively; and now the affair of David Kemball dropped out of his mind. For thirty minutes he worked on the Mafia report, which gave a detailed estimate of the number of gaming halls, casinos, slot-machine rackets and protection rackets controlled or influenced by the Mafia. Each of the countries in the Police Conference was preparing a similar report and early in the autumn there was to be a full scale international conference of the Crime Haters, when the danger from the Mafia would be thoroughly discussed.

Now *that* was a conference to look forward to.

It was seven minutes to ten when he finished, and leaned back again. It was surprising how much such a concentrated effort took out of him, and he let his whole body sag as it recharged. At five minutes past ten Childs's door opened and Childs came in, with coffee and biscuits.

'I really haven't got time for that,' Dawlish protested.

'I telephoned to say you would be ten minutes late,' Childs told him. 'They're not likely to start on the minute, this morning.' He placed the tray on Dawlish's desk. 'How has the Mafia report gone, sir?'

'Finished,' Dawlish announced. 'Get it typed, will you—give it a thorough looking over yourself first, of course—and I'll have another go at it tonight.' He poured out coffee, and bit into a biscuit. 'It's pretty formidable.'

'The whole business is,' remarked Childs.

'Did you hear Lancaster on the extension?'

'No,' Childs answered. 'I knew you'd had a call.'

'David Kemball was murdered in the early hours,' Dawlish told him. 'I'm going over to the scene of the crime as early as I can manage this afternoon. Get me out the file on Kemball, will you?' he added as an afterthought.

'Yes,' Childs promised. 'Any clue at all?'

'Not yet.'

Childs hesitated as Dawlish drank his coffee, and then went on: 'Tragic personal life, Kemball's. His first wife died from cancer, she was only twenty-four.'

Dawlish said with a sense of shock: 'I didn't know he had been married twice. Is the daughter...'

'His first wife's,' said Childs. 'She was three when she lost her mother.'

After a pause, Dawlish said heavily: 'Tragic is the word. Poor little kid.' He finished his coffee and stood up. 'Thanks for telling the Powers that I would be late.'

Childs gave a little half-smile, a protective, paternal kind of smile.

Soon, Dawlish was being driven by a police driver to the new H.Q. of Scotland Yard, and at ten twelve precisely he slipped into the small Conference room on the fourth floor. The Commissioner was already on his feet, speaking. A pompous man, it was easy to be influenced by this and to underrate his ability as an organiser. A steward took Dawlish to a seat in the small theatre which was used as a lecture hall or conference room. It was a place of light and air conditioning, sponge rubber and tubular steel comfort.

'... the ugly but unavoidable fact that crime is on the increase,' the Commissioner was saying, 'and the Home Secretary is convinced that this is to some degree our responsibility. Naturally, when I am confronted with such a charge, I refute it, but I think it is time that we, at the Yard, examined our own record, our own methods, I might say, our own consciences . . .'

Just a pep talk, thought Dawlish. He let his mind drift to Kemball, the particular case on which he had helped Dawlish, and the bravery he had shown. He had parachuted down into a blazing forest to bring out a woman who had been kidnapped and imprisoned in a woodman's hut.

No part of this reverie prevented Dawlish from hearing all that the Commissioner was saying; he could whistle and ride, as it were: keep several balls in the air at once.

A messenger approached Dawlish and placed a note in his hand. The Commissioner obviously noticed this, but it did not stop his discourse.

'. . . As policemen we have a very grave responsibility . . .'

Dawlish unfolded the note.

'We think we know why Kemball was killed,' it said. 'Please come at your earliest. Childs.'

CHAPTER THREE

MOTIVE

Perhaps the Commissioner's voice really did boom louder as Dawlish closed the door very gingerly. Dawlish took out a card and wrote across it: *'My apologies, Commissioner. Very urgent investigation calls me,'* and handed this to the messenger. 'See that the Commissioner gets this as soon as he has finished.'

'Very good, sir.'

Dawlish nodded, and hurried off. His car was outside but the driver, assuming himself free for the rest of the morning, had gone off. Dawlish had a key, got in and drove back to his office. It was a to-and-fro kind of morning. It was something else, too. Every now and again a case cropped up which seemed to gather momentum with uncanny speed, until it caught Dawlish and everyone involved in a breathless chase. This could be one of those cases. Certainly Lancaster had convinced Childs of the urgency of this new development.

Childs was in his, Dawlish's office, at the telephone.

'Yes ... I'll tell him ... Oh, hold on, please, he's just come in.' He handed the telephone to Dawlish, saying clearly: 'Inspector Labollier of Paris, sir.'

Labollier was fairly new to the Crime Haters, and had replaced Pierre Crystal who had died in the course of an investigation which had started off in the same indirect way as this.

'Hallo,' Dawlish said. 'I was going to call you later.'

'Later can be too late,' retorted Labollier, in good but accented English. 'I understand you are always ahead of events, never behind them.'

'Someone has been pulling your leg,' Dawlish replied.

'Someone has been pulling...' began Labollier, and then his voice changed and he laughed. 'Now I understand! We shall see, M'sieur Dawlish. I am very concerned now about the *passeports*.' He used the French pronunciation.

'What's new about them?' asked Dawlish.

'I have some evidence to suggest that over two thousand false French passports have been produced, and are for sale. And before you are facetious, please—yes, there are over two thousand bad men in France who could use these. But our concern is, who might use them to come illegally into France!'

'I know the problem,' Dawlish said. 'We raided a hotel two days ago and found three French passports which didn't seem genuine. They're on the way to you now.'

'I shall be *very* glad to see them. Tell me—have you learned more of the problem in England?'

'We know there are far too many false British passports about,' Dawlish said. 'We haven't made your kind of wholesale rate.'

'So, we are the first to be affected so much,' said Labollier. 'Goodbye for now, then.'

Dawlish replaced the receiver slowly, to find Childs looking at him intently, questioningly. The glance they exchanged told each of the other's doubt about Labollier's ability but Dawlish simply made a note of Labollier's statements and then asked:

'So what was the motive for Kemball's murder?'

Very carefully, Childs answered. 'He was investigating an insurance fraud for Global Insurances, and he had just reported that he believed that the frauds were being perpetrated by switching identities—that false passports were used as identification after certain accidental deaths.'

The office was very quiet after Childs finished, and Dawlish moved to the window which had a view of Westminster Bridge, the river, the Embankment. There was light and movement and a world which seemed so far away from the one he was hearing about now.

'A variation of the passport switch,' he echoed. 'Is that it?'

'Yes.'

'Where did we get the report from?'

'Global Claims Department. There was a letter in Kemball's pocket, and Lancaster immediately checked. It's not yet wholly clear,' went on Childs. 'There's hardly been time to get all the details, but the principle seems to be that there would be car, sea or air accidents, and some of the bodies would be unrecognisable, but passports were used to prove identity. In a great number of cases, big insurance claims were paid out.'

Dawlish looked blank.

'And so?'

'One of the reportedly dead men, on whose death a hundred thousand pounds had been paid, was seen alive,' Childs answered. 'Kemball was asked to investigate for Global. They know he made some progress, and he told them he thought he was on the threshold of a very big discovery which connected false passports with big insurance claims.'

'Did he name anyone?' Dawlish asked.

'No.'

'He never liked to talk unless he was sure of the situation,' said Dawlish. 'So it seems possible that someone knew that he had discovered too much about these passport frauds and killed him.'

'That's the obvious possibility,' Childs agreed.

'Yes,' Dawlish hesitated. 'Labollier said they have evidence of the existence of two thousand false French passports.'

Childs breathed: 'My God!'

'Yes indeed.' Dawlish sat on the corner of his desk, big and powerful, surprisingly relaxed. His eyes, a piercing blue, contemplated Childs and he was silent for a long time. At last, he decided:

'I'll go over to Hallows End Garden Suburb straight away. Who's there?'

'The Divisional people, and Lancaster—Lancaster got on to Global as soon as he found the letter in Kemball's pocket, of course.'

'Yes.' Dawlish stood up, and repeated. 'Yes. I'm wondering

22

whether to alert everybody about the passport angle in this murder, or——' he broke off, and gave a broad, brilliant smile. 'I'll wait! *You* collect as many reports as you can about the forged passport situation in other countries, though. We may need an emergency conference.'

'I'll see to it,' Childs promised.

Dawlish looked about the office, reminding himself how little he had been in it, or was likely to be in it, that day. There was far too much for one man to do, and Childs did a magnificent job, but he couldn't be expected to keep up the pressure much longer. Younger assistants were needed, and Kemball might have been just right to take charge. There was another man who had promised well, Gordon Scott, but Scott had recently talked of resigning so that he could go to New York and get married. There was far too much to do, yet the Home Office was never enthusiastic about paying well to keep this part of police work at its peak. It was astonishing how blind officialdom could be. If it were possible to stamp out, or even substantially to reduce, crime on an international scale, it would help the police to concentrate on their national crime problems. The whole police world was far too harassed, today, by the ease and frequency with which criminals moved from one country to another.

A large supply of forged passports would make it even easier and more frequent.

'Is anything troubling you, sir?' Childs asked, uneasily.

'I just had a glimpse of how big this case could become,' Dawlish said. 'Was Kemball working alone?'

'He refused any assistance, yes,' said Childs. 'In fact, I think the only time he worked with anybody was when he worked with us, sir.'

Dawlish was thinking of that when he reached Hogarth Avenue. Hallows End Garden Suburb lived up to its name. It was such a pleasant part of Greater London, and with the sun shining on the trim lawns and flower-beds, the well-kept and newly-painted houses, it had, he thought, quite an idyllic touch.

Dawlish turned off the main road with its parade of shops and tall, terraced houses, into the north end of the 'S' which formed Hogarth Avenue. Then, reaching the middle sweep of the 'S', he saw the cars, the crowd, the photographers and Press men, the policemen in uniform at the doors of two houses.

One of these was a small bungalow, with roses beginning to flame from well-tended bushes. The other was a two-storeyed house: Kemball's, he felt sure. As he passed the bungalow, wondering why the policemen were there, he saw a child at the window, her face distorted with grief. A middle-aged woman stood just behind her, hands outstretched.

So that was Kemball's daughter.

As his car drew up, Lancaster appeared at the doorway of the house, and newspapermen and photographers drew nearer. Someone called: 'That's Dawlish,' and he heard others echo his name. Cameras flashed and one on a tripod whirred for the now universal television.

Chief Superintendent Lancaster was a burly-looking man whose double chin and jowl gave him something of the look of a bloodhound: florid of face, he came forward, wispy greying hair blowing in the wind.

'Hallo, Superintendent.'

'Good to see you, sir.' They shook hands.

'Hold that, please,' a photographer called out. 'Could you turn a little this way, Mr. Dawlish? ... Shake hands again, please ... just one more.'

As the photographers finished, a short, very fair haired man at the front of the crowd called out:

'Does this mean there's a foreign angle, Mr. Dawlish?'

'*Foreign?*' a man echoed.

'He means international,' another called. 'Crime Haters stuff.'

'Does it, sir?'

'There could be,' Dawlish conceded. 'Otherwise, why should I be here?' He smiled pleasantly, then turned with Lancaster and went indoors. 'The body's been removed, I take it?'

'To the Hallows End morgue, yes,' Lancaster said. 'There's no doubt of the cause of death. I've some pictures, if you'd like to see them.'

'Like' was hardly the word, but Dawlish followed Lancaster into a room on the right. This ran the whole width of the house, with windows at one end and French windows at the other, leading to a lawn. Several shelves were filled with china, while on three large squares of the wall hung some exceedingly good miniatures. For the rest, there was a table, a couch and several comfortable armchairs.

On the table were spread several glossy print photographs.

Dawlish went forward to look at them. Three were of head and shoulders, one taken from above, one each from either side; and three were of the whole body taken from roughly the same positions. All of them showed the gash; the way the blood had spread; and the round, rather boyish face.

'One slash was enough,' Lancaster said.

'So I see. And there's so little sign of spattering that he was probably asleep. The bedclothes weren't disturbed, and there was his head dent in the pillow.'

'Couldn't have done *that* if he hadn't been,' agreed Lancaster. 'Cold-blooded devil. He just came in and slashed.'

Dawlish looked away and moved towards the personal belongings—a watch, keys, some loose silver—the sad relics of a man who had been vigorously alive only a few hours before. Obviously there was nothing of great interest to the police here. He nodded, and they went out.

'What would you like to see first, sir?'

'Evidence of the search,' answered Dawlish.

Lancaster took him from room to room, showing everything that had been moved or in any way disturbed. There were indications of a very thorough, careful and orderly search: things which had obviously been moved a little way; dust marks showed that even the miniatures had been shifted slightly out of line. Kitchen, a small dining-room with sideboard, cupboards and chairs, a downstairs cloakroom, two small bedrooms upstairs; everywhere bore the hallmark of the practised searcher.

Then, they turned to the child's room, and Dawlish saw the parachutist, dangling down. Because he had dropped from an aircraft so often he had a special interest in this, nodding appreciatively at the perfection of the model.

'Even got the boiler suit kind of uniform right,' Lancaster remarked.

'Yes. Odd thing for a girl to play with,' Dawlish said.

'Shows you don't know much about children,' Lancaster retorted. 'Boy or girl, if it's anything to do with your father, you like to have it around. He was in the parachute regiment, wasn't he? I'll bet that child *sees* the parachute toy as her father. Probably imagines it's him every time she lets the thing fall. Like to see it work, sir?'

When Dawlish nodded, Lancaster fingered the twine or cord of the parachute, and Dawlish saw that there was a string attached to the lintel of the door from a hook which stuck out about three inches. A little catch in the top of the parachute, rather like the catch of an umbrella, retracted under pressure. Suddenly, the parachute began to open slowly and the 'man' began to fall. He was supported by the attachment which fastened to the door cord. At last, the tiny feet touched the floor and the legs bent, the little model fell gracefully on to his shoulders and the parachute collapsed as gently a few inches away.

'Just like the real thing, sir, isn't it?'

'Uncanny,' agreed Dawlish. 'How's the child?'

'In a *very* bad way, sir. They can't do anything with her.'

'Sedative?' asked Dawlish.

'The doctor who was called in says he'll give her one to-night, but he thinks it better to let her cry her grief out.'

'Hard-hearted or a wise man,' mused Dawlish, half to himself. He placed the parachutist at the back of the door, seeing that there was enough string, or twine, to let it fall a long way, and looked about the room. It was untidy, with pencils, crayons, books, dolls' clothes, paper and toys, but was obviously spotlessly clean. He wondered whether the dead man or the daily woman kept it so. On a tiny dressing table were photographs of two women in the same folding frame; Kemball's two wives?

At last, Dawlish moved across the landing, where a policeman stood at the door of the room in which Kemball had been killed. There were the bloodstained pillow and sheets, and bloodstains on an off-white Indian carpet. Apart from that the room was normal except that it also showed signs of having been very thoroughly searched; pictures had been moved, drawers left open, chairs were obviously out of position. On the side table was a photograph of a dark-haired woman with quite lovely eyes and pleasant features.

'His wife,' volunteered Lancaster. 'Did you see the similar photograph in the child's room?'

'With her true mother?' hazarded Dawlish.

'Yes, sir. And now——' Lancaster took out his handkerchief and trumpeted loudly. 'Gives me the willies to hear that child cry,' he went on. 'Always hated to hear my four bellow, and today I'm nearly as bad over the grandchildren. But they don't let 'em cry so much these days. Don't know whether it's a good thing or bad.'

'How many grandchildren?'

'Seven,' answered Lancaster proudly. 'Four boys, three girls. And my youngest daughter will have the chance to even out the sexes, she's expecting her first in a couple of months.'

'Hope it's a girl,' said Dawlish. He stood looking round the room, and then stared very straight at Lancaster, but did not speak for several minutes. Lancaster began to get restive.

'What do you make of the search?' Dawlish asked at last.

'Very thorough and expert, sir. As I said before.'

'You notice he's moved all the miniatures,' Dawlish pointed out.

'*Very* thorough, sir.'

'The reason for it would seem to be that he was looking for something very small,' Dawlish mused.

Lancaster was startled. 'I hadn't ...' he began, and then he nodded. 'Yes, of course. *Very* small, sir.'

'And he didn't keep Kemball alive long enough to ask,' said Dawlish. 'I don't understand it.' He straightened up. 'Ah well, worst jobs always come last.'

'*Worst* jobs, sir?'

'Yes,' said Dawlish. 'The child might be able to help, you know.'

Lancaster looked flabbergasted.

'But I've talked to her, sir! She didn't hear or see a thing. I had her on my knee and asked every question I could think of. You don't have to talk to her again.'

'But I'm going to,' said Dawlish, starting for the door. 'By the way, has she had her parachute toy since she went next door?'

'Well, no,' answered Lancaster after reflection. 'We couldn't let anything go until everything had been fingerprinted. Only the child's and the father's prints on the parachutist, as it turns out, but ...' he broke off, as Dawlish picked up the toy. When he spoke again his voice held more than a touch of reproof: 'If you'll forgive me for saying so, sir, I don't think there's the slightest chance of getting anything out of Kathy. And I don't think it's fair or right to harass the child unless there *is* a chance that she can help.'

'If I were in your shoes I would say exactly the same thing,' replied Dawlish. 'Would you care to come with me?'

'I'd rather you saw her alone,' Lancaster said stiffly.

Dawlish nodded, murmured: 'I'll see you before I go' and

went out of the room and down the stairs.

The moment he was in the garden he saw Kathy Kemball still at the next door window, looking at her own house. She no longer seemed to be crying but her face was a mask of grief.

CHAPTER FOUR

KATHY

'Hallo, Kathy,' Dawlish said, in his normal speaking voice.

The child stood in front of him, very still. She did not speak or even try to answer. Her eyelids were swollen and her eyes bloodshot, but the pallor of her cheeks and the almost bloodless hue of her lips shook Dawlish badly. The neighbour, Mrs. Halkin, was also in the room. She did not speak either, her expression being one of powerlessness in the face of grief.

Dawlish went up to the child. 'I used to know your father a long time ago.'

A spark of interest showed in Kathy's eyes; but still she did not speak.

'We once jumped from the same aeroplane,' Dawlish said tentatively.

She looked up at him, her attention held.

'He was a very brave man.'

'Of course he was brave,' Kathy asserted. 'I know that. Besides, Mummy told me.'

'Did she, then,' said Dawlish. 'I'll bet she loved him a lot.'

'Oh, she loved him *ever* so much, she used to tell me so,' declared Kathy. 'She loved him tre-tre-tremendously!'

'I bet he loved her, just as much,' remarked Dawlish.

The child stared at him as if puzzled for the first time, and her lips tightened and her eyes seemed to grow rounder. She didn't answer at first, and Dawlish did not persist with the questions but put his hand to his pocket. She did not look away. He drew out the toy parachutist and rested it on the palm of his hand.

'I've never seen a toy like this,' he stated flatly.

'That's mine!' she cried, her voice high and sharp. 'That's mine!'

'I know it's yours.'

'My daddy gave it to me!'

'Yes,' repeated Dawlish, letting her take the toy. 'I thought Mrs. Halkin might let it hang behind your door tonight. We could easily get the cord and fasten it.' He turned to the woman. 'Couldn't we, Mrs. Halkin?'

'Well, yes, I'm sure my husband will ...'

'I don't want to stay here!' cried Kathy. 'I want to go home!' She clutched the parachute toy tightly to her breast, and began to cry quite helplessly. Tears began to stream down her face. Another woman appeared, another neighbour, and Mrs. Halkin let Dawlish out of the room, with Kathy's crying following them.

'Oh, it's heart-breaking,' Mrs. Halkin said huskily. 'I can't understand why the doctor didn't give her a sedative at once. It's a shame, it really is a shame. He *says* he will tonight, but the poor little thing's cried her heart out. She really has, Mr. Dawlish, she's cried her heart out. She's as welcome as the flowers in May to stay here, but if I can't do anything with her, and she keeps on crying, what's the use? Do you know,' the woman went on, striking a pose, 'she was better with you than anyone who's been here today, you calmed her somehow. That ridiculous Superintendent kept asking her questions, as if she could have heard anything in her sleep. As I stand here, she's been better with you than anyone.'

Dawlish looked at the earnest face very thoughtfully, and said: 'You've been very kind to her, and I'm sure you're right, she should have a sedative. And I don't think she should wake up within sight of her house, do you?'

'Oh I don't!' Mrs. Halkin cried fervently. 'I really don't. If you would arrange something I would be ever so grateful.'

'I'll do what I can,' promised Dawlish.

When he went back to Kemball's house, he found Lancaster a little subdued. All the routine was over, and most of the reports were now in. Kemball's death had been from the single knife slash; according to the autopsy report, he had been in very good health and very fit. Dawlish went over the details, and then said:

'We've got to get that child away, Lancaster.'

29

'Don't I know it! But believe it or not she hasn't *any* relatives. Not to say relations. There are two second cousins in Nottinghamshire and her step-mother's parents in Canada, but they're very old. So unless we sent her to a home ...'

'Let's think about it,' said Dawlish.

Lancaster knew him well enough to realise that he had already been thinking a great deal, but the superintendent was so preoccupied with the question on his own mind that he did not make any comment.

'She didn't give you any information, did she, sir?'

'Only that her mother or her step-mother told her of her father's bravery,' replied Dawlish rather vaguely. 'Lancaster ...'

'But your questioning her didn't really help, did it?' persisted Lancaster, as anxious to be reassured that Dawlish hadn't succeeded where he had failed.

'We're going to find out whether it helped or not,' Dawlish said drily. 'That car accident in which her step-mother was killed—do you know anything about it?'

'I checked that there were multiple fractures of the body and the cause of death was cerebral haemorrhage, following a collision with a stationary truck. Instantaneous death, sir.'

'Yes. Get the coroner's report and the pathologist's report and the police statement, will you?' asked Dawlish. 'Just routine,' he added, almost hurriedly, as if he were expecting Lancaster to protest. 'You'll put in your report to your Commander in the usual way, won't you?'

'Of course, sir—and a copy to you.'

'Thanks,' Dawlish said. 'This—ah—passport business with Global, by the way. Whom did you see?'

'The Chief Claims Officer,' answered Lancaster. 'Be sure I will follow it up very closely.'

'I know you will,' Dawlish said. 'And I'll keep in touch.'

'Thank you, sir,' said Lancaster, and then he hesitated for a few moments before going on: 'This is a little difficult, sir, with the overlapping of departments, but—er—who *is* to look after Kathy Kemball? We can't leave it in the air, can we?'

'We most certainly cannot,' Dawlish agreed. 'Leave her to me, will you?'

'Very good, sir.' Lancaster was expressionless, either in approval or disapproval.

Dawlish went into the sunlit street and past the ghoulish crowds. Only two or three cameras clicked. He was conscious of towering inches above most of the people near by, as well as of some frank and some covert glances, as he made his way to his car. His driver was standing at the door and opened it as Dawlish came up.

'So you're back,' Dawlish remarked.

'Yes, sir. Sorry about this morning, I quite thought you would be away all the morning. As a matter-of-fact ...' the driver was being over-fussy, obviously more than a little guilt-stricken. 'I've heard that the Commissioner's conference is likely to continue throughout the day.'

'Then I might catch up with it,' Dawlish said drily. 'Straight to my home, please.'

'Very good, sir.'

Dawlish sat back, a great number and variety of thoughts passing through his mind, most of them focused on Lancaster's remark about overlapping. The superintendent was quite right. This was a case for the Metropolitan area police, and his, Dawlish's, responsibilities were to liaise, not to usurp. Lancaster had been prompt and very good in consulting him, but the case did not really come under his, Dawlish's, jurisdiction. He had never known a case which was so near the dividing line.

And that wasn't the only problem; there was Kathy herself. He was actually striding across the foyer of the luxury block when it struck him that Felicity, his wife, might not be at home. The sense of anticipated disappointment was very great, and he was drumming on the side of the lift as it stopped.

He went outwards; and Felicity came forward.

'*Oh!*' he exclaimed.

'Pat!'

'Darling, thank goodness you're in!'

'But Pat...'

'Aren't you in?'

'Darling, my hair...'

'It is very nice hair,' said Dawlish, 'and if you can't make another appointment before you're going to need it done, I'll wash it for you myself.' He took her arm as he stepped out of the lift, and there was a faint ting! of sound as it was summoned from below. He held her lightly as they went across the passage to their pent-house apartment. 'I can't say how glad I am I caught you,' he went on, taking out his keys.

'You really should let me know when you're going to get

31

home early,' Felicity said vexedly.

He knew in that moment that he had been ill-advised to behave in such a boisterous way. Felicity was very touchy about her hair, had a special hairdresser and, he knew, was anxious about a dinner party a day or two ahead. She was usually completely understanding of any of his problems, and put up with a great deal, but now—how wise would he be to tell her what was in his mind? He stood inside for her to pass, and she went straight into the hall and to the telephone. He watched her. She was tall, with an unusually good figure; now, she wore a tiny hat over fair hair which looked the fairer because it was beginning to go grey. Her hairdresser would put that right, of course! She had a pleasant speaking voice and fine, green-grey eyes, now sparking a little in frustration or annoyance. Not beautiful by many standards, there was some quality about her face which had always made her beautiful to him.

And she was particularly so, now.

'Thank you—M'sieu Hibbert, please.' She looked across at Dawlish without smiling, a sure sign that she was put out. 'Eh? ... Mrs. Dawlish ... Yes ... very well, will you find out if you can postpone my appointment for an hour?' There was a long pause and in it Dawlish would normally have gone up to her and played the fool, but this time he could not bring himself to. The waiting was prolonged, and Felicity began to frown. 'I'll bet he can't help at all,' she said to Dawlish. 'I ... oh, hallo?' Her face and her voice brightened, hopefully. 'Eh? Oh ... *when*? ... oh, very well ... I'm really sorry, but I ...'

Dawlish strode towards her.

'You go,' he urged. 'I can wait.'

Poor Kathy Kemball, she could wait, couldn't she?

'Just get back as quick as you can,' he urged.

'... I really can't make it,' Felicity finished. 'Do tell M. Hibbert how sorry I am.'

As Dawlish moved away from her, she put down the receiver and for a few moments they stood looking at each other. She was still vexed, obviously, and he had gone cold, chilled, inside, not knowing now how best to approach her with what he had in mind. It should have been done in a good mood on either side; lightly, almost gaily, but that wasn't possible now; there was no point, really, in raising the subject. He went towards her again and kissed her lightly on the cheek. 'I'm sorry, sweet. Ring up and say you'll be there. My little idea can wait.'

'What little idea?' she wanted to know.

'I was going to go out for a drive. Out to Richmond, perhaps, or even as far as Epping,' he announced evasively. 'It's such a lovely day...'

'Pat,' she interrupted. 'What is it, really?'

She knew him too well, of course; knew that he was dissembling; and she would not rest until she had wormed the truth out of him. But as he watched her, he thought: how impossible, how absurd, to think of Kathy, here. They had their life, a pleasant, social, gay one when he wasn't deeply involved in a case. There was nothing about it to raise him to the seventh heaven, but it was very enjoyable and not at all taxing. And there were some other facts. Felicity was only a year or two short of fifty, set in her ways, a wonderfully loyal and kind-hearted and *good* person, but...

She put a hand on his arm, with great gentleness and appeal.

'I'm sorry I was piqued,' she said in a much warmer voice. 'I've been running late all day and didn't think I'd make the appointment in time, anyhow. And bumping into you at the door was quite a shock.'

He was smiling, and already feeling much, much better, for her expression had softened, and so had her eyes. Then, swift and sharp her expression changed again; alarm flared.

'Pat!' she cried. 'Nothing's the matter, is it? Nothing serious? Nothing's gone wrong?'

'Not for us,' he said reassuringly. 'I'm on the fringe of a case which might prove to be ugly and difficult, but that's a long way from certain yet. No. Let me tell you what has happened, and...'

'Have you had lunch?' asked Felicity, switching suddenly to practicalities.

'No,' Dawlish answered, and suddenly realised he was hungry. 'That's a good idea. What about some bread and cheese and coffee, while I tell you what's been going on.' He took a bottle of beer out of the larder and stood, leaning against the draining board, aware of the intentness of Felicity's gaze whenever she turned to look at him. He told her in some detail and it seemed a long time before he stopped.

The bread and cheese was all gone; so was the beer. He now sat back in a kitchen chair, with Felicity on the other side of the primrose yellow table. He wasn't quite sure how she had taken the story.

'The idea wouldn't have occurred to me if she hadn't seemed to take to me as a kind of uncle. I soothed her, without knowing how. You could soothe her too, I think. She hasn't a relative who counts, and the neighbours don't seem able to handle her in her present mood, not even the kind Mrs. Halkin. If she came here for a few nights, and it didn't work out ...'

'Pat,' interrupted Felicity, 'at least we must try.' She stood up and leaned towards him, placed her hands on his shoulders and looked intently into his eyes. 'You didn't think I'd want to, did you?' she asked, half marvelling, half reproachful. 'How long do we have to be married before you know me, darling?' When he didn't reply but just smiled up at her, his relief—his gladness—showing in his eyes, she pressed his shoulders more firmly, and bent down and kissed him. Then she added: 'I only hope she takes to me. Children take queer likes and dislikes. Can you come over with me, to see her?'

She had barely finished when the telephone rang; it was Childs, very anxious that Dawlish should go to the office at once.

'All right,' Felicity said, 'I'll go to Hallows End by myself, darling. Keep your fingers crossed for me!'

'I shall give thanks for you,' declared Dawlish, much more affected than he sounded. 'Call Lancaster at Hallows End, he'll give you Kathy's address.' He rounded the table and gave her a hug and a kiss which drove the breath out of her body, and turned and hurried away.

CHAPTER FIVE

PASSPORTS BY THE HUNDRED

Childs came into Dawlish's office just as Dawlish entered by the main door, and his brown eyes, often sad and doleful, were bright with rare excitement.

'I hope I didn't call at a bad time, sir.'

'I should have been here much earlier,' Dawlish said. 'But what's so urgent?'

.'The Foreign Office is nearly going mad,' said Childs, and it was so unlike him to make an extravagant statement that Dawlish knew this must be very nearly true. 'They have discovered over sixty passports, all originally issued to Commonwealth citizens, all allowing free passage in and out of Great Britain. The only thing wrong is that each number is one which has already been allocated to someone else. Two different people have the same passport number, in other words. There was a query over a passport held by a Pakistani living in Notting Hill, and one of the clerks came upon the duplication.'

'Well, I'm damned,' Dawlish said heavily. 'Who's been after us to make you want me so urgently?'

'Mr. Montgomery Bell,' answered Childs. 'The Minister at the Foreign Office.'

Dawlish said: 'What about our report for the next Crime Haters meeting?' Almost before he finished, he snapped his fingers, pausing for hardly a second before going on: 'We want copies of the reports from all the delegates, including Labollier's, as quickly as we can get our hands on them.'

'I've telephoned Labollier for a copy of his,' said Childs. 'I wondered whether we should alert all the Conference nations about it?'

When Dawlish didn't answer, he went on:

'I know everyone's been alerted to the danger but they haven't been told that these passports with genuine numbers are in circulation.'

'No, they haven't,' Dawlish agreed. 'Yes, we'd better alert everybody. And check with the secretariat about the possibility of a meeting to discuss passports in general and frauds involving them in particular. This could become very big indeed. Did the Minister go into much detail?'

'He didn't say the obvious thing,' said Childs.

'You mean that a large sequence of numbers might have been taken from the Passport Office?' suggested Dawlish.

'That's what I most fear,' said Childs.

'Is Bell coming here?' Dawlish wanted to know.

'I said you'd call him as soon as you came in.'

'Thanks,' Dawlish approved. 'I'll get him while you send the general warning out.' He was already looking down a confidential list of Whitehall Government Office numbers, came upon Montgomery Bell's name, dialled and asked for Bell himself.

'The Minister is deeply involved, sir,' a secretary answered. 'Who . . .'

'This is Deputy Assistant Commissioner Patrick Dawlish,' Dawlish announced formally.

'*Mr. Dawlish!*' cried the man who was obviously keeping Bell's casual callers at bay. 'Just one moment, please.'

Dawlish did not have to hold on for long, but there was time for him to recall what he knew of Montgomery Bell. This particular Government, and so this particular politician, was comparatively new, and Bell himself was one of the youngest ministers. His was a theoretical and professorial reputation, without much practical evidence of results to judge him by. Dawlish, who was not directly controlled by the Foreign Office but had some responsibility to it, as he had to the Home Office, had never come into direct contact with him. Nothing had happened since he had taken office to tell Dawlish whether, with regard to the Crime Haters, he could rely on this man's support. This was a good time to find out, and it was much better that Bell should have made the first approach.

At last he came on to the line. 'Mr. Dawlish, Bell here. I'm very glad you called.'

'I would have earlier . . .' Dawlish began.

'I'm quite sure you called as soon as you could,' said Bell, 'I've a private exchange line I'd like to use while we're talking. My secretary is ready to dial on it. If you will ring off . . .'

This was on-the-ball efficiency which Dawlish liked, and it also told him that Bell was very concerned indeed. Almost as soon as he hung up the bell rang, and Bell went on as if there had been no interruption.

'Your man Childs was very cagey, but I didn't get the impression that he was surprised. Did you know we were going to have some funny business over passports?'

'We knew we were having some,' Dawlish said.

'Forgive me—but if you knew, why weren't we warned?' asked Bell.

'You would be the last people we would tell until we knew that was going on,' retorted Dawlish promptly.

'Why on earth should you say that?'

'Why do you prefer to speak about it on private lines so as to be sure we're not overheard?' countered Dawlish.

There was a momentary pause before Montgomery Bell gave a faint, obviously amused chuckle; Dawlish began to feel that this was a man he could easily like.

'Keep me in touch from now on, won't you?' Bell asked.

'Yes,' promised Dawlish. 'What is your particular worry, sir?'

There was only a brief pause, during which Dawlish adjusted himself to the fact that an inquiry which had started less than a day ago, had suddenly flared up into proportions of some magnitude.

'I've reason to believe that a block of numbers was passed on to the forgers by a Passport Office official,' said Bell. 'False numbers can be easily detected, but duplicates of real ones can't, unless a detailed search is made and the numbers circulated to all immigration officials at ports and airports, a very difficult task.' Then Bell went on in a sharper voice: 'You *do* realise how very serious this could be if done on a widespread scale, don't you?'

'It could make nonsense of the Immigration Act, let every criminal we want to keep out of Britain in and turn Passport Control into a nightmare,' Dawlish declared at once.

'I should have realised that you would know,' said Bell, almost grudgingly. 'There are some indications that a sequence of numbers up to a thousand in all was photographed with details of their present holders. I could have you visit the Passport Office and see the evidence, but the Senior Officer in charge feels that such a move could scare off any member of the staff involved.'

'Do you know you can trust the Senior Officer?' interrupted Dawlish, very quietly.

There was a pause, before Bell answered: 'I think you and I should have a talk as soon as possible, but my diary is so full that I can hardly squeeze another half hour in for several days. Unless you eat breakfast early?'

'I'll eat it tomorrow at whatever time you like,' offered Dawlish.

'Thank you. Seven-forty-five then, at my office.'

'I'll be there, thanks. But first, who is the suspect?' asked Dawlish.

'The man on the staff involved, you mean?'

'The man who might be,' Dawlish interpolated.

'I take your point. He is an Alan Crayshaw—CRAYSHAW —and he lives at 41 Hammond Avenue, Clapham Common,' answered Bell. 'I think the evidence is fairly conclusive. He is known to have a small Leica camera, cigarette lighter size, known to have used it. He has access to the files where the allocations are kept. These are old numbers—we don't use the same number again ever, you know, and there is a real probability that the original citizens who were given the numbers are either dead or unlikely to travel often. But do you think it's wise to start anything until you've had a chance to investigate?'

'Did you read about the murder of a man named Kemball this morning?' asked Dawlish.

'My dear chap! Unless it's foreign news, I hardly ever read anything in a newspaper. My secretary marks things I should read. I would never have believed the amount of work involved in a comparatively minor ministerial post—oh, never mind. What about this man Kemball?'

'He was inquiring into an insurance fraud in which faked passports were involved,' said Dawlish.

There was a long silence, broken only by the sound of his own breathing and the breathing of the man at the other end of the line. Then:

'You're the policeman, Mr. Dawlish,' Bell said. 'I'll be advised by you.'

'Thanks,' Dawlish replied with real gratitude. 'I'll report tomorrow at breakfast!'

When he rang off, he gave himself time to ponder for a few moments, then pulled a London Street directory towards him and looked up Hammond Avenue. It was a turning off Clapham Common Raad, and he should have no difficulty in finding it. He was pressed for time, however, for it was now after four o'clock, and passport officials often went home early.

Quite suddenly, he was faced with an overwhelming temptation—to go there himself.

He should really send one of his senior officials to interrogate Crayshaw, and at once, for the man had to be questioned tonight. With such a ruthless crime as a murder of David Kemball involved, it was folly to delay a minute. If he did this, however, he would have to brief another man, and briefing him thoroughly wasn't going to be easy. He, himself, had the background of the puzzle at his fingertips, and in half-an-hour might learn more from Crayshaw than one of his officers could learn in days. The great sense of urgency about this case seemed to increase all the time, and if he lost even an hour it could be disastrous.

Once he had talked to Crayshaw he could pass the whole story on to a chief inspector or a superintendent who would automatically liaise with the other C.I.D. men. Childs came in, just as he had made up his mind. The older man looked at him knowingly and understandingly.

'Are you going out, sir?'

'Yes.' Dawlish had written down Crayshaw's name and address. 'I'm going to this place. If I'm not in touch again by half-past six, set the usual wheels rolling, will you?'

'I will,' promised Childs. 'Will you have a look at this before you go?'

He placed two sheets of paper, each typewritten in double-spacing, in front of Dawlish, who sat back and read.

This was the teletype message which Childs proposed to send to every national police force in the world. It was precise and to the point, but long enough to have left nothing vital out. As he read, he thought again: Childs is going to be a damned hard man to replace.

He handed the draft back.

'Get it off as soon as you can.'

'It'll be on its way inside the hour,' Childs assured him. 'One other thing, sir.'

'Yes?'

'If this is *really* on a big scale it could——'

'I know,' interrupted Dawlish. 'That is what the Minister is worried about, too. It could sabotage the whole system of passports and immigration control, and give us a hell of a lot of trouble we don't want.'

'That's precisely it, sir,' Childs said. 'And if it's on a really big scale then someone really familiar with passport control needs to be brought in. It's very tricky indeed, and it isn't easy to learn the ins and outs of it in twenty-four hours.'

Dawlish eyed him levelly.

'Go on,' he urged.

'I know just the man,' Childs told him. 'Chief Inspector Patandi of the *Records* Office at the Yard. He was seconded to the Passport Office a few years ago when the problem of Indian, Pakistani and Jamaican immigration was first raised, and was there until a few months ago. We could do with him here if *Records* would release him.'

'Will you ask at once?' asked Dawlish.

'Be much better if you did,' Childs countered. 'They'll take it much better from you, and if you would approach the Assistant Commissioner C.I.D. so that *Records* couldn't argue, it would help.'

'Yes, I suppose so,' Dawlish said rather heavily. 'Have you had any trouble with co-operation lately?'

'Some,' Childs answered frankly. 'We always get what we want, sir, but one or two senior C.I.D. officers are a little obstructive, and I don't think we should risk delay over this, do you?'

Dawlish stared at him very straightly, and then said: 'Have you a report on this affair in the making?'

'I've notes on which I could base one, and it wouldn't take long,' answered Childs.

'How long?'

'Once the Mafia report is out of the way, only a few hours.'

'Do it just as soon as you can, will you?' asked Dawlish.

When he left his office, very soon afterwards, he was scowling in subdued anger. He worked on the simple philosophy that if a job wanted doing it should be done at once, and that red tape should be cut without a second thought. Not every senior policeman agreed. There were pride, prejudice and protocol to overcome, and protocol and red tape were everpresent at the Passport Office. This investigation was going to be bad enough in its own right, without any kind of obstructiveness.

As he took the wheel of his car he remembered the conference he had left so abruptly, and the Commissioner's prosy appeal to the senior officers to look into their own departments and their own attitudes so as to make sure they were not themselves making the investigation of crime more difficult.

'The Old Man might have a point,' Dawlish said aloud.

Then he pushed everything out of his mind and concentrated on what he was going to say to Alan Crayshaw.

41 Hammond Avenue was a pleasant, tree-lined street of terraced and semi-detached late Victorian houses. All were three stories high, of grey brick with stone facing, all had slate roofs, their small front gardens protected from the pavement by a brick wall, itself capped with slate. Dawlish reflected that it was the late Victorian version of the estate at Hogarth Avenue, Hallows End. Larger, more solid, less bright and

spacious here, there was nevertheless colour in the gardens and beauty in the trees. Number 41 was about halfway along the avenue, which stretched from Clapham Common itself to another street which was practically identical. Dawlish drove round and about the neighbourhood to get his bearing, found a parking place only fifty yards away from Number 41 and then walked up to the front door. He knocked briskly, but nothing happened. He pressed a bell, and waited, but heard no sound.

Then, as he pushed back the letterbox in an attempt to see inside the hall, he heard a cry which was quickly suppressed: a cry which sounded very much like a woman, calling '*Help!*'

CHAPTER SIX

THE KILLERS

Dawlish lowered the flap very slowly, his ears strained now to catch the slightest sound. He heard what might have been a scuffle, a gasp, a blow; then silence settled. He rang the bell for a second time, keeping his finger on the push for much longer; stopped; then banged on the knocker so loudly that people passing in the street glanced round. There was no further sound from inside Number 41.

Clearly but not too loudly, Dawlish muttered: 'They must be out.' He turned and walked down the steps to his car, going slowly, as if disconsolately. Several cars, two cyclists and a dozen pedestrians were in sight, forerunners of the rush-hour density. It was nearly half-past five, and Crayshaw would surely be home soon. He was likely to have a warm reception, too! Dawlish felt sure that a woman in the house, presumably his wife, was being held captive; that whoever held her was waiting for Crayshaw. And he had vivid mind pictures of David Kemball with his throat slashed; swift, sudden death.

He got into the car and took the first turning to the left, then left again. This was a street parallel to Hammond Avenue, and there was room to park. He parked and took the next left, on foot. As with most streets of this period, there was a service alley running between the back gardens of Hammond Avenue and those of the road which ran parallel. He turned into this. Each garden had a wooden gate, marked with a number. In less than three minutes from the time he had left the front door he was pushing open the back gate of Number 41. And his luck was in, for there were four apple trees, all in full leaf, between himself and the house. Beyond the trees was a beautifully kept vegetable garden, peas, runner beans and spring greens, beets with their leaves already turning colour, carrots, onions with their slender stalks bent over, soft fruit bushes, the fruit a pale green. On the other side was a bed of roses, and, in the middle, a grass path, edged and protected with a plastic edge liner.

Once past the trees, Dawlish knew, he would be visible from the house itself.

He studied it, swiftly but thoroughly. It was tall and narrow, and there was an extension from the first floor, which no doubt housed the kitchen and the scullery. And there was a window in the main house, close to a side door which must lead to the kitchen. If he kept close to the wall on the right leading to the extension building, he was less likely to be seen. He moved towards this. Walking was easy, for a path ran close to the wall, obviously there to provide good access to the rose bed, which had recently been turned and worked over with compost.

It was clear that Alan Crayshaw of the Passport Office cared for this garden, and the work put into it had been a labour of love.

Dawlish looked upwards, but saw no one at the back windows, no indication at all that he had been seen. As he made his way along the narrow path, his mind worked almost mechanically. The sounds which had come from downstairs had been so loud that if there was anyone on the first or second floors, they would surely have been aroused. The back door would probably be locked, but one of the sash windows on the first floor was open a few inches at the top. He reached the wall of the extension and found a stack of wood close to it, put a foot on the wood and climbed up. It was easy enough to get on to the roof. The greatest danger was that someone in the back gardens or at the windows of other houses would see him. The roof was sloping, but he reached the main house wall; then he dislodged a tile, and it fell, making a sharp crack

42

of sound as it hit the paved yard.

He went very still. If the noise attracted attention, it would make people look in the garden first, but once they recognised a roof slate they would know whence the danger threatened. He leaned forward and opened the window much wider, making hardly a sound. It was tricky to put a leg sideways, step on the windowsill and then haul himself head-first through the top half of the window, but he manoeuvred his body with great dexterity and soon was inside the room, standing almost on his head. There was a bed on the left, and he eased himself in its direction, twisting his body so that he was able to fall on to it.

Springs creaked, but not too loudly.

He shifted himself round until he was sitting on the bed, then stood up. No noises came from inside the house. He went to the window and looked on to the paved yard; there was the slate, broken into several pieces, but no one appeared to have noticed. He turned towards the door, which stood ajar. The room itself was overcrowded, with the bed against the wall, covered with a gold coloured satin bedspread, a big mahogany wardrobe and a dressing table with sizeable wing mirrors.

He opened the door wider and peered out on to a narrow landing with several doors leading from it. The light, from a window halfway down the stairs, was subdued. No one was in sight. He stepped on to the landing, soundlessly, and looked into the other rooms. There were two bedrooms, one large and one small, a bathroom and a separate W.C. Another narrower flight of stairs led upwards, but no one was likely to be up there, or he would have heard indications. Whether he was right or not, he had no time to find out, for he heard a sound at the front door. Hardened though he was to danger and to crisis, his heart began to beat fast. The sound was metal on metal; key in the lock.

The door opened and a man stepped in.

He was of medium height, rather lean, rather dapper. Crayshaw, of course. As he closed the door he took off a narrow brimmed bowler hat and hung it on a peg on a hall stand; and at the same moment he called out:

'I'm home, Rose.'

There was no answer.

Dawlish saw his greying hair, the small round bald patch, the pale, rather sharp-featured face. The man did not glance up but looked along the passage at the foot of the stairs. He called out again, more sharply.

'Rose! I'm home.'

Again there was no answer, and he walked from the hall, along the passage itself. Dawlish started down the stairs, keeping to one side so as to lessen the risk of creaking. His heart had steadied, but he was on edge, remembering the savagery with which Kemball had been killed. If this man got within range of a knife or dagger . . .

Crayshaw stopped suddenly, and drew in a hissing breath. Obviously he was staring at something out of Dawlish's sight. Dawlish went further down the stairs, tread by tread.

A man said: 'Come in, Crayshaw,' in a very quiet voice.

Crayshaw raised his hands, as if to ward off some evil thing.

'Don't try to run or you'll get this knife in your back,' the speaker went on.

Crayshaw, still standing absolutely still, said hoarsely: 'Where is my wife?'

'Never mind your wife, I want to talk to you.'

'I won't take another step until I know where she is,' Crayshaw said, in the thin voice of a frightened man.

There was silence, and Dawlish reached the foot of the stairs, crouching. If Crayshaw turned he would see him through the banisters, but there was only one direction for the man to look: and that was forward.

'Don't be a bloody fool,' the invisible speaker said. 'Do you want to get her throat cut? or yours?'

Crayshaw said in a voice which Dawlish could hardly hear: '*Where is my wife?*'

'She's in the kitchen,' the other answered.

'I want to see her.'

'Come on then. You can't see through brick walls or wooden doors.'

'Bring her here,' Crayshaw muttered. 'Oh . . . no!' He broke off with a screech, and Dawlish saw the glint of a knife, *saw* it bury itself in Crayshaw's shoulder. Crayshaw staggered, backwards at first, then drunkenly forward.

Dawlish peered over the banisters in time to see him being dragged into a room by a broad, thickset man, dark-haired and swarthy-faced. Just behind the doorway stood a taller man, fair-haired, English-looking. The first man gripped the handle of the knife in Crayshaw's shoulder, and pulled it out.

44

Crayshaw gasped with pain.

The taller man gripped him by the wrist and thrust him further into the room, then moved after him. The darker man wiped the blade on a white cloth suddenly stained vivid crimson from Crayshaw's blood. Now everyone was in the room and the door was half-closed. Dawlish ventured closer.

'What—what—what have you done to my wife?' Crayshaw muttered in anguish.

'She wouldn't stop shouting for help, so we bound and gagged her,' the tall man replied. 'That's nothing to what we'll do to you if you don't answer my questions.'

Crayshaw didn't speak.

'Did you tell Kemball anything?' the man asked sharply.

'Who—*who*?'

'You know who I mean; David Kemball.'

'I—I don't know anyone named Kemball!'

'You had a drink with him last night, at the Rose and Crown,' the other said with absolute certainty.

Crayshaw gasped: '*That* man.'

'You knew him, didn't you? Don't lie to me.'

'No, I didn't,' Crayshaw interrupted shrilly, and Dawlish warmed to his courage. He was terrified, but did not cringe, and his defiance was still sharp and stubborn. 'I don't know him, I'd never seen him before.'

'Then how come you were drinking with him?'

'He forced himself on me!'

'Don't lie!'

'What's the use of asking questions if you won't believe the answers I give you?' demanded Crayshaw with a surge of anger born of his fear. 'He practically forced me to have a drink with him, I tell you. He——' Crayshaw paused, but the other did not interrupt, and stood patient for the first time. 'He came over to me and asked me what old passports I had for sale today, and I knew that he knew.'

So,' the other man said. 'You told him about the numbers.'

'I didn't tell him a thing!'

'Yet you talked to him,' the tormentor said. 'You were seen.'

'That's right,' Crayshaw muttered. 'He wanted to know how many passport numbers I'd given you. God knows how he knew.'

'Did you tell him?' demanded the other.

'No,' Crayshaw answered thinly. 'I didn't. I didn't admit

anything.'

'If you're lying——'

'I'm not lying!' Crayshaw made a sound, probably a sharp intake of breath. 'I told him he could have the details if he was prepared to pay for them.'

'My God!' the man exclaimed. 'You've got a nerve! After all the money we've paid you!'

'I told him I wanted £500,' Crayshaw went on in that thin stubborn voice. 'If I'd asked for £5000 it wouldn't have been too much.'

'Anyone who gets greedy...'

'Don't be a fool,' Crayshaw retorted. 'I wouldn't have become involved in this in the first place if I hadn't been greedy. I'm sick to death of it, and I wish to God I'd never started. They've even begun to ask questions at the office!'

'About you?'

'About some old passport numbers,' Crayshaw replied.

'Did you say anything?' demanded the man who was so full of questions.

'Of course I didn't say anything!' Crayshaw answered, in mingled fear and resentment. 'But they know something's wrong, and——' He broke off, and again Dawlish sensed that he was very much afraid.

This was the moment Dawlish judged right to go into action. He pushed the door back with a bang, and had a vivid glimpse of the scene.

Crayshaw, standing near his wife, who was bound to a chair and gagged; the dark-haired man behind him, his right hand raised with the knife in it; on the far side of the room the tall, fair man, staring at Dawlish in open astonishment.

That was the moment of acute danger.

Dawlish saw the man with the knife change his position, knew that the knife was coming at him, saw the blade glint, ducked and hurled himself forward. The knife flew over his head. The dark-haired man, who had astoundingly swift reflexes, kicked out. But Dawlish was so big that he was able to grip the other halfway up the calf before the hard shoe cap landed. He tugged. The man, standing on one leg, went crashing, head towards his accomplice, who whipped out a gun. Dawlish saw Crayshaw move.

He would never know whether he could have reached the man with the gun in time to save himself, if Crayshaw hadn't

46

moved. As it was, Crayshaw flung himself forward. There was the sharp crack of a shot, followed by a gasp. Crayshaw began to fall, but he fell forward, on to the man with the gun. Dawlish saw the dark-haired man reach for his knife. Before it was in position Dawlish struck him across the face, sending him reeling sideways, then crashed his fist into a yielding jaw. Instantly, he spun back to Crayshaw and the man with the gun.

The man was trying to push Crayshaw away, trying desperately to get his gun free, but he had no chance at all. Dawlish hit him fiercely and hard. The gun dropped. Crayshaw rolled over, and did not move. Dawlish stepped back a pace, breathing harshly—the woman's face seemed to force itself into his line of vision. She was staring at her husband and there was utter despair in her eyes.

Dawlish went towards her, watching the other two men, convinced that neither could threaten any danger for at least five minutes. He took out a knife and cut the cord at her wrist, then cut through the scarf with which she was gagged. He drew her arms forward on to her lap as he said quietly: 'I'll get a doctor at once. Try to take it easy.'

He did not think she had heard him, as she stared at her husband. He went forward, turning Crayshaw's body over very gently, looking into his face. He was glad that, standing thus, he shielded the woman at least for a moment, for there could be no doubt that Crayshaw was dead. The bullet had taken him in the neck, and the blood from the torn jugular vein was pulsing out.

Into those moments of dread silence there came a heavy banging on the front door.

CHAPTER SEVEN

THE PRISONERS

Dawlish cradled the dead man in his arms, and said to the woman over his shoulder: 'See who that is, please.' She did not seem to hear him. 'Go quickly,' he urged. 'Whoever it is can send for the doctor.'

He heard her move. He sensed her leaning over his shoulder, to peer at her husband's face. It was very strange; even macabre. He heard a rustle of movement, and knew that his last words had registered with her; she was desperately anxious for a doctor. God! What a case. First the orphan child, now the tragic widow. He rested Crayshaw on the floor, and stood up. A red chenille tablecloth was spread over a long dining table, and there was a glass vase of flowers in the middle; artificial roses. He moved the bowl to a side table, and pulling off the chenille cloth, draped it over Crayshaw, drawing it over the man's face. He felt overwhelmingly anxious to save the woman from seeing the gaping wound in the neck.

He straightened his own jacket and felt something wet and sticky. He clenched his teeth, knowing that it was blood. He heard a man's voice some distance off, and at the same time saw the tall fair man stir and open his eyes. The fair-haired man seemed to be unconscious.

'If you move,' Dawlish said to the man who had shot Crayshaw, 'I shall break your neck.'

The man went still.

The voice was nearer now, the man who had called out was in the passage.

'. . . better have a look for myself, ma'am, before I send . . .'

Rose Crayshaw pleaded: 'Send for a doctor, please send for a doctor.'

The door opened a little wider and a policeman appeared, the top of his helmet brushing the lintel of the door. The woman was just behind him, almost hidden.

'Please,' she was saying. 'Please.'

The policeman stood stock still, looking about him. His expression was almost comical; astonishment, alarm, and then slowly, authority, all followed one another almost as if he switched them on and off. He was a broad man with a very broad face and dark eyes. His gaze rested on Dawlish, on the draped figure, on the two men, and then back at Dawlish. Slowly, a new expression showed; recognition. He gulped.

'It—er—it is Mr. Dawlish, sir, isn't it?'

'Yes, officer. Get a police surgeon here at once. And'—he almost said 'murder' but checked himself—'a full team.'

'I understand, sir. Are you . . .'

'I'll be all right,' Dawlish said. 'Is there a telephone here, Mrs. Crayshaw?'

She was now in the doorway, looking towards the spot where her husband had been. He seemed to see her clearly for the first time: a much older-looking woman than he had expected, with lined face and tragic, tragic eyes.

'Is there a telephone, Mrs. Crayshaw?'

'There's one at the corner, sir,' The policeman told him. 'I'll use that.' He turned and hurried off, his footsteps loud and decisive.

Mrs. Crayshaw held on to the door, tightly, while she looked past Dawlish to the floor. Shorter than the policeman, she could see only the covered head and shoulders of her husband. She moistened her lips, and her pale face became even paler. Dawlish moved but the table was in his way and he couldn't reach her in time to stop her from falling. Her knees doubled up and she crumpled rather than fell. The murderer moved with sudden, ferocious speed, hurling himself at Dawlish's back. Dawlish, half-aware of what the man might do, bent forward, and his assailant went flying, thudding against the wall. The dark-haired man moved at the same time, not towards Dawlish but towards the passage.

Someone was coming along it.

'Look out!' roared Dawlish.

The dark-haired man disappeared. For a second there was the sound of his footsteps; and then silence. Dawlish reached the door in time to see him crouching in front of a man with a woman behind him. Had the dark-haired man held his knife he might have used it, but he was weaponless. Dawlish looked over his head at the newcomer's face.

'A policeman asked me to come and look after Mrs. Crayshaw,' the man blocking the passage said. 'What's going on?'

'If you'll go to her, I'll explain everything later,' Dawlish promised him, and he added words which were not wholly familiar to him for he used them seldom and so sparingly. 'I am a police officer, and I will be grateful for your help...'

It was surprising how quickly and how smoothly things moved from then on. The neighbour and his wife took Mrs. Crayshaw next door, the man carrying the unconscious woman. Within three minutes a police patrol car arrived with two policemen, and there was no longer the slightest need to worry about the man who had shot Crayshaw.

'Hold him for a murder charge,' Dawlish ordered. 'The

49

C.I.D. will be here soon, presumably?'

'There'll be a team here in a few minutes, sir, with Chief Inspector Herbert in command.'

'Good. I'll go and wash,' Dawlish said.

He went into the kitchen, which had a big old-fashioned sink, ran hot water and washed his hands and face, then took off his jacket and sponged it as clean as he could. There was a small, framed mirror. He looked into it, and saw a brown smear on his shirt: dried blood. Well, that would have to wait until he got home. Home. He thought of Felicity and wondered how she had fared at Hallows End, with Kathy Kemball. Finished, he felt suddenly as if his legs would give way under him, and he moved a few feet and dropped on to a kitchen chair. He wasn't dizzy so much as nauseated; and of course he was suffering a little from shock. What couldn't he do with a cup of tea? He heard more footsteps and voices, and knew that the murder squad had arrived. He could go, now—and he could have Herbert send to the Yard for interrogation. It was a job which he, Dawlish, could do better than anybody, but he had so far exceeded all regulations that he might be well advised to play strictly by the book from now on.

Chief Inspector Herbert, whom he had never met before, was a tall, dark, youthful man with very bright grey eyes. He was a brisk man, too, well on top of his job.

'May I ask whether this *is* a Crime Hater's job, sir?' he asked.

'It overlaps.'

'I shall be very happy to accept your guidance, Mr. Dawlish!'

'I'd like you to get the prisoner to the Yard, and have him charged with murder,' Dawlish said. 'I was an eye-witness. And I'd like to inform Superintendent Lancaster, who is in charge of the Hallows End murder case.'

'Are the two connected, sir?'

'Very closely,' Dawlish answered. 'Keep a tight hold on the dark-haired chap. He knifed Mr. Crayshaw.'

'You're certainly collecting a bag full,' Herbert remarked. 'Is there anything I can do for you personally?'

'No,' said Dawlish. 'No, I'll be at my office or at my home. I'd like to know the names of the two prisoners as soon as possible.'

'I'll soon get them, sir,' said Herbert confidently.

Dawlish went out into the street and saw the inevitable crowd of on-lookers, drawn as by magic to any sensational happening. There were no photographs and, as no one asked questions, presumably no reporters. Among the several policemen keeping the approach to the house clear was the big man who had come just when he was needed. Dawlish stopped by his side.

'Everything all right, sir?'

'It will be. What brought you, Constable?'

'A neighbour reported seeing a man force entry through a back window, sir, and dithered a bit before telephoning us.'

'Oh, did they?'

'Yes, sir. A big man apparently.'

'Well, those two chaps had to get in somehow,' Dawlish said, with a faint smile. There was an answering knowing smile in the policeman's eyes, an 'I know who it was but I won't tell, sir' expression. 'How did you get in?'

'The next-door neighbour had a key, sir.'

'I see. What's your name?' Dawlish asked.

'Green, sir. P.C. Green.'

'You were very prompt,' Dawlish said.

'Very glad I *was*, sir.'

'Keep inquiring after Mrs. Crayshaw, won't you?'

'I certainly will,' the policeman promised.

Dawlish nodded and went on. Half a dozen small boys followed him, but did not get too close. He took the wheel of the car and eased it out of a space made small by recently parked vehicles. Before long, he was driving along Clapham Common Road, unnoticed—or at least unrecognised—which was exactly as he wanted to be. It was a glorious evening with clear skies, and the sun was spreading gold over the green leaves of the trees. The Common was seething with youngsters playing cricket, tennis, golf, rounders, netball—everything they could set their energies to. For anyone who knew nothing of what had happened, the scene was idyllic. Only a few young lovers, with their brazen eagerness, were as yet beneath the hedges and the trees. The spate of workers from the city and West End had thickened, as the traffic heading towards the centre of London thinned out. It was half-past six. He drove over Lambeth Bridge, and went straight to his flat. A doorman pressed the lift button for him.

'Is Mrs. Dawlish in?'

'I haven't seen her, sir.'

'Thanks.' Dawlish nodded, and went up.

Felicity was not in. Feeling vaguely disappointed, Dawlish poured himself a whisky and soda and crossed to the wide windows. All he could see were the faces of two people who had suffered such a loss today. He could—perhaps he should—be rejoicing. He had caught two of the men involved, by to-morrow the police might be well on the way to solving the problem of the false passports, but somehow, he doubted it. His drink half-finished, he sat down and pulled the telephone towards him, dialling his office.

Childs answered, almost at once.

'You shouldn't work all night as well as all day,' Dawlish said, almost reprovingly.

'I had to see everything through, sir,' said Childs. 'I'll be off now that you've called. That man Patandi's down with 'flu, and not likely to be back for a week. I'm afraid he can't help us in time.'

'We'll manage,' said Dawlish, more confidently than he felt.

Childs said: 'I expect so, sir,' and went on: 'I've briefed the night duty men, and they'll call you or me if we get anything of importance during the night.'

'Right. Any problems?'

'It's been very quiet here,' said Childs. 'I understand things haven't been so quiet for you, sir.'

'Quiet certainly isn't the word,' Dawlish said. 'I'll see you in the morning—— Oh! Did I tell you that I'm having breakfast with Mr. Bell at the Ministry at 7.45?'

'No,' said Childs, and chuckled. 'I'm glad we're not the only ones who get up early! Good night.'

'Good night,' echoed Dawlish.

He rang off, and finished his drink, wondered how long Felicity would be and whether he should call Hallows End to find out. He decided not to, went into the bedroom and caught sight of his bloodstained shirt. He stripped it off and put on a clean one; it would have been quite a shock for Felicity to have seen that. He went into the kitchen, surprised to find himself hungry, and suddenly realising that there wasn't likely to be a substantial meal tonight, then saw a joint cooking in the oven. For ever Felicity! He went back to the big room, and picked up the evening newspaper. There was a picture of David Kemball and of Kathy, but not one of him;

thanks be for small mercies! He read a rather perfunctory account of Kemball's murder, and was turning over the page when the telephone bell rang.

Felicity?

He picked up the receiver.

'This is Patrick Dawlish.'

'Mr. Dawlish,' said a rather exaggeratedly cultured voice. 'I would very much like to come and see you.'

Oh, no, Dawlish almost groaned; and he said aloud without enthusiasm: 'Who is speaking?'

'I am known as Smith.'

'*The* Smith?' asked Dawlish drily.

'*A* Smith,' the man retorted equably. 'It is of course an assumed name, and I shall be disguised when I come. It is a very private matter I wish to discuss, as well as a very urgent one.'

Dawlish relaxed his hold on the telephone, but there was no relaxation in his body. Suddenly, he felt sure that he knew what this call was about; and as suddenly, he was convinced that he had a long, long way to go before the case of the false passports was finished. He recalled the Minister's tone of voice when he had asked if Dawlish understood how significant the case might be. These thoughts passed very swiftly through his mind, but he paused long enough for the man who called himself Smith to go on rather more sharply.

'Are you there, Mr. Dawlish?'

'Yes, I'm here,' Dawlish said heavily.

'What time would be convenient for you?'

'No time at all, Mr. Smith,' answered Dawlish.

'I do most seriously urge you to change your mind,' Smith insisted.

'I don't change my mind very often,' retorted Dawlish. 'Not so often, as a matter of fact, as I change my passport.'

The man at the other end of the line gave a soft, amused chuckle.

'You guess very accurately,' he said. 'Shall we say eight-thirty?'

'No,' repeated Dawlish. 'I shall not be free.'

'Mr. Dawlish,' Smith interrupted in a sharper voice, 'you must not be foolish. You already know this is a matter of extreme urgency, and I am most anxious to discuss certain aspects of it before you see the Minister in the morning.'

He paused.

Dawlish thought astonished: Before I see Bell. *That* secret's out! He became suddenly very, very wary, and felt close to real alarm. Bell had gone to a lot of trouble to make sure their telephone call could not be heard on an extension or switchboard, yet this man talked with such confidence that he seemed almost to have a right to know about the appointment.

'I simply wish to discuss the matter under review with the hope of helping in the widespread inquiries,' Smith said. 'And —ah—I wish also to acquaint you with some of the advantages of your position. This—ah—particular affair could be of great benefit to you. A matter of a hundred thousand pounds, in fact. I really do think that you should see me.'

Very slowly, Dawlish said: 'I'm beginning to agree with you, Mr. Smith. We'd better say ten o'clock.'

'Good!' exclaimed Smith. 'Ten o'clock is rather late, but will do very well. Now a word of warning, Mr. Dawlish; don't do anything rash, will you? I shall be *very* well protected. I shall come in peace and goodwill, mind you, but if you should attempt to detain me or do violence——'

He held the last word for a few seconds, and then rang off.

CHAPTER EIGHT

THE VISITOR

Dawlish replaced the receiver, slowly, as if to move quickly would do irreparable damage. As it rested on the cradle, he stared at it, the speaker's last words seeming to come from it, echoing.

'I shall be very well protected. I shall come in peace and goodwill, mind you, but if you should attempt to detain me, or do violence——'

Years ago, long before he had become a policeman, and while he had fought tenaciously against crime and criminals as a lone wolf, Dawlish had often come into conflict with such men; had been offered huge bribes to join the criminals or at least to keep silent. And time and time again, he had been threatened, far more viciously than this. But he was now a Deputy Assistant Commissioner, a senior policeman, and his position, his seniority, should have placed him above both corruption and threat. For the man had not simply threatened him, Patrick Dawlish; he had threatened, and had attempted to bribe, the Metropolitan Police Force.

And he knew of tomorrow's breakfast appointment with the Junior Minister at the Foreign Office. So his spies, his informers, were everywhere.

'Everywhere,' Dawlish said aloud, and his mouth was dry. 'Everywhere.' He stood up slowly and went back to the kitchen, took out a bottle of beer and poured it into a glass. His movements were slow and deliberate, but his mind was going at racing speed. The unknown man who called himself Smith had a very great confidence: the confidence of a man who felt absolutely sure that he could get what he wanted.

Dawlish drank deeply.

'*Ah*,' he breathed aloud. 'Everywhere. But where is everywhere?'

That was the vital question: where did Smith have his informers? How far in Government Offices did his tentacles spread? Whatever else, *that* had to be found out. The passport business was grave enough in itself, but it was beginning to look as if it were only one of many ramifications of the activities of the man who called himself Smith. Aloud he said: 'Must find out a lot more.' Then he thought: 'Felicity and that child should be here by ten o'clock.'

He glanced at his watch; it was nearly eight, certainly past time he heard from Felicity. When Smith came, he, Dawlish, would be with Felicity, perhaps helping with Kathy. He should never have arranged for Smith to come here.

Nonsense! he decided. The only problem was how to cope when Smith arrived. What kind of protection would he bring? What...

'My God!' gasped Dawlish, and he stood absolutely still: as if he were frozen. The possibility that Smith had intercepted Felicity and the child slashed into his mind. If that had happened, if they were Smith's prisoners, then it would explain the man's overwhelming confidence. And it would also explain why Felicity had not come. For a few seconds he could not move, the shock effect was so great. Then, he began to relax, but there was the ache of foreboding in his bones.

The telephone bell rang.

He jerked around towards it, hand stretching out, and then hesitated. It rang on, *burr—burr—burr*. He picked it up half fearful. 'Dawlish.'

'Oh, Pat!' exclaimed Felicity. 'I *am* glad I've caught you.'

He sat down heavily in the chair in which he had talked to Smith, the strength in his legs going. His heart hammered with the relief as he responded:

'I'm glad you caught me too, a long time ago.'

'What—Oh!' She laughed. 'Idiot, Pat, I'm at Ted and Joan's, I thought it better to take Kathy there as they've children of the same age. They are all playing together, as if they were old friends.'

'Thank the Lord for that,' Dawlish said fervently. 'It was a good idea.'

'I thought so! Pat, darling, I think I'll stay here for the night,' Felicity went on. 'Kathy seems to have taken to me and it would be best if I were here when she wakes up in the morning. Do you mind?'

'It's another happy thought,' Dawlish approved. 'I've a Mr. Smith coming to see me at ten o'clock, and the discussion may last quite a while. So it's all working out for the best.'

'Do I know Mr. Smith?' asked Felicity, with faint suspicion.

'I doubt it,' Dawlish said, and there was a slight pause before Felicity went on: 'I can come round and get your dinner if you'd like.'

'Nonsense,' Dawlish interrupted. 'I'm going to cut off some slices of whatever you've got in the oven, and raid the larder for whatever's there. Have a very good night, sweet. And bless you for taking Kathy so well.'

In a thoughtful tone, Felicity said: 'She's a very unusual child.' Then more briskly: 'Pat, Ted wants a word with you.'

Ted Beresford, one of Dawlish's oldest friends and associates in the days when Dawlish had been a freelance crime fighter, had settled for stockbroking in the City with his now near-matronly wife. They had a house overlooking Regent's Park, and it was a perfect temporary sanctuary for Kathy Kemball.

'Hello, Pat,' Ted boomed.

'Hi, Ted,' said Dawlish. 'Take special care of Felicity, won't you?'

'Is that necessary?' Ted asked, lightly.

'I think so.'

'I shall protect her as if she were my own,' Ted assured him. 'Have no fears, Mr. Deputy A.C. What kind of progress are you making?'

'So so,' Dawlish answered, truthfully.

'Anything I can do?' asked Ted.

'Nothing except look after Felicity and the child,' Dawlish told him. 'Do you want me for anything in particular?'

'Only to find out if you wanted me for anything in particular,' Ted countered. 'Happy hunting, old man!' He rang off, as if very pleased with life.

In a much more light-hearted frame of mind Dawlish went into the kitchen, took out the roast, which proved to be a piece of sirloin, the potatoes surrounding it cooked to a delicate brown, carved several slices of the beef, turned the potatoes into a vegetable dish and plumped them on the kitchen table. He ate with gusto, his mind working very clearly now that the main cause of anxiety had been relieved. He could call Childs and alert his own department and the C.I.D. In some ways it would be better. But if he did that, then official action would be required against Smith. If only he knew about the man at this stage, if Smith, for instance, thought that he might be susceptible to threat or bribe, then he could learn a great deal. With the two prisoners, there was a good official start. Quite suddenly, and positively, he decided to handle Smith by himself.

He finished the beef, found some apple pie and a carton of cream in the refrigerator, poured the cream over the pie and ate with renewed gusto while a kettle boiled. He made himself some coffee, and drank it while he put the dishes in the dishwasher and cleared up the kitchen. By the time he was through it was half-past nine. He washed, then went into the main bedroom and put on a velvet smoking jacket and some slippers, sat back in the easy chair by the telephone and skimmed the rest of the news in the evening papers. The certain thing, he told himself, was that Smith would be very clever, probably very cunning. And if he wanted either to frighten or bribe Dawlish, then his thoughts would surely turn to exerting pressure in a way that would render him an easier victim.

It was ten to ten when the front door bell rang.

Dawlish dropped the papers and sprang to his feet.

'He's early,' he said aloud, and with eager anticipation, went out of the room, into the hallway, and opened the door.

Two women, young women, stood there.

Dawlish was so surprised that his mouth dropped open. They were both young and very pretty, one a blonde and one a brunette. They stood a little apart from each other, smiling up at him, and he gulped, and recovered, and told himself they must come from Smith; they were part of his 'protection'.

'Hello,' he said. 'The Misses Smith, I presume?'

The blonde, who had a merry face and blue eyes, gave a pleasant little laugh, and then darted past him into the hall. He half turned trying to grab her, and the brunette, who had glowing brown eyes, darted past on the other side. She laughed, too. Dawlish looked along the passage and saw no one. He drew back into the hall, closed the door and gave a double twist to secure it, then went into the living room. Neither of the girls was there and he could not hear a sound. He glanced into the kitchen; no one was there. That left only the two bathrooms and three bedrooms. He went into the hall and towards the main bedroom door when a piercing scream almost deafened him, and it came from the bedroom. Another scream followed, and then he could distinguish words.

'I'll kill myself ... you've betrayed me! I can't face the shame ... I'll kill myself ... I thought Dawlish was a man of honour ... I'm going to have his baby and he won't even help ... I'll kill myself.'

He pushed the bedroom door wide open.

The blonde, mother naked, was writhing on the bed. The brunette was standing by the window taking photographs one after another in rapid succession and Dawlish sensed when it swivelled round on him. There was no flashlight just the click, click, click; she hardly gave herself time to focus the camera. The blonde continued to scream and to writhe—and suddenly she appeared to see him, sprang off the bed and with her arms wide open, ran to him.

'Pat!' she cried. 'Pat, promise to look after me! Swear you will!' Quite suddenly she was flinging herself bodily at him, her arms tightening round his neck as the camera went click, click, click.

For the first few seconds, he was flabbergasted. Then he realised exactly what they were up to; at any moment the door might be broken down, or the brunette would run off with her pictures. There was a tape-recorder too, or it wouldn't be worth the blonde's while to scream so vehemently. They ex-

58

pected him to be so utterly astounded, so alarmed, so anxious to quieten the screaming that he could think of nothing else.

The blonde was still clinging to him like a limpet, and now she was screaming at the top of her voice, face upturned, mouth wide open, eyes glaring. There wasn't a hope of pulling her off, but he knew exactly what to do. He eased his right arm and crooked his elbow, then slapped her on the bottom with all the force he could command. She was so astounded and so stunned that she relaxed her hold. He prised her away, and slung her beneath his arm. She kicked and swung her arms but there was nothing she could do to free herself. The brunette stuck to her task, click, click, clicking all the time and edging towards the door. With his free hand Dawlish clutched a pillow—and, blonde under one arm, pillow raised, he leapt towards the brunette, hurling the pillow with all his force at her head and shoulders. She stumbled. He went after her, gripping her by the back of the neck so tightly that she could hardly move. She clutched the camera as he pushed her towards the door. The blonde was now gasping for breath, and the movement of her arms and legs was much less wild.

He put her on the floor and opened the door, pushed the brunette out and grabbed the camera. Then he bent down and picked the blonde up, great hands spanning her slim waist, and carried her into the hall. Neither of the girls seemed to have any breath left in their bodies. He slammed the door on them, and stalked back to the bedroom, gathered up a dress, stockings, brassiere and panties, screwed them up into a bundle, went back to the door and flung them outside.

As he closed the door again, he wiped the back of his hand across his forehead.

'After that, I need a drink,' he said aloud.

He poured out a whisky and soda, and sank into the telephone chair. The camera, he soon saw, had a tiny built-in tape recorder, and that didn't surprise him at all. Still a little breathless, he leaned back and contemplated the telephone, suddenly plucked it up and dialled *Information* at the Yard. He was answered at once.

'This is Deputy Assistant Commissioner Dawlish,' he announced. 'A few moments ago there was a naked blonde and a breathless but decently-clad brunette outside my apartment. Send a car to make sure they don't make any more nuisance of themselves, will you?'

The Inspector in Charge echoed: 'A *naked* blonde, sir?'

'Powerfully naked. If she's still not wearing clothes she can be picked up on an indecency charge. Hurry, will you?' He rang off on the other's faint 'Yes, sir' and sipped his drink.

Almost at once, the front door bell rang again. He took his time going towards it, being careful to keep the door on the chain. He could see one man standing there, but there might be others on either side.

'Who is it?' he demanded.

'My name is Smith,' the man announced. 'I have an appointment.'

'Not now,' said Dawlish. 'The deal is off. No one who can try a crude trick like a dumb blonde and a tape recorder-cum-camera is worth even five minutes of my time. What do you think this is? A music hall?'

Dawlish closed the door but did not move away. Almost immediately there was another ring. After a brief pause he opened the door again.

'Mr. Dawlish,' said Smith. 'I apologise for that particular intrusion. I still think we should have our discussion.'

Dawlish hesitated, and then drew out the safety chain and let it fall, keeping his foot just behind the door as he drew it backwards. He was quite prepared for a rush from the other side of the doorway, but there was none, and the man stepped in. Dawlish closed the door on the double lock as the visitor passed him then led the way into the big room.

The man who called himself Smith was in the early or middle forties. Dawlish studied the eyes and the face, noting signs of clever disguise, quite sure that his real appearance was very different from the one he showed now. He wore a dark grey suit, a pale grey tie, pale grey socks and black shoes.

'What will you have to drink?' asked Dawlish.

'You're very kind. May I have a brandy?'

'Yes, of course.' Dawlish poured brandy into a small bowl-shaped glass, handed it to the man and demanded: 'How did you find out about my meeting with the Minister at the Foreign Office?'

'In the same way that I find out anything I want to know,' Smith said. He gave a quick, pleasant smile, and went across to the big window. 'What a wonderful view!' He inhaled the bouquet with appreciation, and then sipped. 'Every principal and every secretary has a price, Mr. Dawlish. Every policeman too. I have come here for one reason only: to find out what your price is.'

He turned his back on the window, and faced Dawlish frankly, obviously waiting for him to respond.

'And you sent the two girls to take the wind out of my sails so that you could drive a hard bargain,' Dawlish said at last.

'I have known many a man unnerved by even simpler tricks,' Smith observed. 'I know now I made a mistake, however, and in my world mistakes cost money. I offered you a hundred thousand pounds, Mr. Dawlish. I now double that offer. Two hundred thousand pounds, tax free. Only a *very* foolish man would turn that down.'

CHAPTER NINE

A VERY FOOLISH MAN

It was not easy to take Patrick Dawlish's breath away, but for the second time tonight, this man had come near to doing just that. He was so poised and sure of himself and there was little doubt that he was fairly certain that Dawlish would accept the offer, and quickly come to terms. Dawlish, sitting opposite, studied him closely. There were the familiar signs of make-up, but make-up could not alter the bone formation, although skilful shadowing might appear to do so. Normally it could not alter the eyes, but there were some drugs which could temporarily change the colour; Smith's were hazel. He had a very direct look, which Dawlish decided was partly due to the gum at the corners of his eyes and lips. The result was vaguely puppet-like.

'Two hundred thousand pounds, tax free,' Smith repeated. And when Dawlish did not respond he went on earnestly: 'If it would be an inducement, the money—part, or all of it— could be placed to your credit in the United States.'

'Ah,' remarked Dawlish. 'No currency problems? No struggles with the Treasury?'

'Ours is an international organisation, Mr. Dawlish.'

'Passports and such like,' Dawlish murmured.

'That is only one aspect of our operation, I assure you.'

'I can believe it,' Dawlish said, and gave what might have appeared to be a baffled smile. 'Almost as widespread and effective as the Mafia.'

For the first time, Mr. Smith smiled. The movement was rather mechanical and did not change the expression of his eyes, but it was very positive, like everything about this man.

'My dear Dawlish! My organisation does not *play* at its affairs.'

'And the Mafia plays?'

'It is very small, comparatively, and——' Smith broke off and frowned. 'I don't think you understand what I have been saying to you.'

'And I don't think you understand what a very foolish man I am,' said Dawlish.

'I do assure you ...' Smith began, then stopped as if he suddenly saw the significance of Dawlish's remark. 'You mean you will *not* accept my larger offer?'

'I mean just that.'

'But Dawlish, surely...'

'I mean that I am a policeman, that I am committed to the organisation known colloquially as the Crime Haters and that the Crime Haters are dedicated to the undoing of all international criminals and international criminal organisations. Didn't you realise *that*?'

Unperturbed, Smith sipped his brandy, chuckled and sat back in his chair.

'Chickenfeed,' he observed airily.

'You mean the Crime Haters?'

'I mean the crime to which you refer. Dawlish, have you *any* idea what I have been saying to you? Have you really been sitting there virtually ignoring me and pondering your own little affairs? Have you——'

'Hush,' interrupted Dawlish. 'I know exactly what you have been saying to me.' He brushed aside an attempted interruption, and went on: 'You have been saying that you have spies in Government departments, in the police force, everywhere. You are saying that you are a world-wide criminal organisation which has grown up over the years without anyone realising that you exist. You have almost certainly based your *modus operandi* on blackmail—only by such means could you obtain the information you certainly have. Oh, yes, you've made yourself clear enough, Mr. Smith. Your organisation must be very powerful indeed. But——'

Smith leaned forward, and this time insisted on interrupting. 'Supposing we talk in terms not of two hundred thousand pounds, Dawlish, but of half-a-million pounds?'

Clearly he considered this the clinching offer. His expression was touched with a kind of smug triumph. He still sat forward, scanning Dawlish's face intently, eagerly. It gained him nothing, for Dawlish's face was blank; there was not the slightest indication on his features of what was going through his mind.

He was, in fact, thinking, as he had not thought for a long time, how much he wished he were not a policeman.

He could deal with this man, as a private individual, in a way that no policeman could or should. He felt like pulverising him. He would like to shake, frighten and if necessary pummel the truth out of him; for Patrick Dawlish, private citizen of independent means, could be infinitely more ruthless than any policeman dared to be. As it was Smith was not only protected by the law which held Dawlish tight as in a vice—one punch on that aquiline nose, for instance, and the whole situation could be changed—but he had come as a negotiator. One drastic move to spoil his disguise and see what he really looked like could make any future negotiations impossible. It wasn't easy for Dawlish to maintain his self-control, but somehow he had to. The smug look of triumph on Smith's face gradually faded, and was replaced by one almost of petulance, although every expression was to some degree controlled by the stiffness of his features due to his disguise.

'Mr. Dawlish, *did* you understand what I said?'

Dawlish looked blank.

'Really! I would never have believed that a man of such eminence could be so obtuse,' said Smith, scathingly.

Dawlish's eyebrows rose.

'You have offered me half-a-million pounds to co-operate with you, and I have refused it. Surely the obtuseness is rather yours than mine.'

'I cannot believe that you would turn down such a munificent offer!'

'Mr. Smith,' said Dawlish, 'someone has brought you up by the wrong standards.'

'But you are not a wealthy man! You have a competence,

63

but without your salary you would have your work cut out to make ends meet! You lost money when you had a pig and fruit farm in Surrey. You simply cannot *afford* to turn down such an offer!' Smith actually looked as indignant as he sounded, and a pale pink glow appeared at his cheeks; but for the paint on them they would have been scarlet.

'So you know all about my private affairs,' murmured Dawlish.

'We know *everything* we need to know!'

'I see,' said Dawlish. 'Mr. Smith, of "Omniscience Unlimited". Tell me, Mr. Smith, what kind of protection have you brought with you? You threatened me, if you remember, that I must not play games.' He stood up with remarkable speed, went to the room door, then the passage door, and pulled it open.

Two men stood there.

He did not know them but he felt sure they were not policemen. As he appeared, each seemed startled, and each shifted his hand to his pocket. Dawlish, moving with quite remarkable suddenness, struck first one and then the other on the side of the jaw and dragged each in turn into the hall.

Smith, full of alarm, had leapt to his feet.

'Back!' ordered Dawlish. He grabbed the men afresh and quite simply banged their heads together with such force that it seemed as if their skulls would crack. Then he opened the door to a small cloakroom and dragged the now unconscious pair into it, slammed and locked the door and dropped the key into his pocket.

Turning, he saw Smith standing with an automatic pistol in his hand. He was obviously badly shaken, and there was a forced violence in his voice.

'That's enough, Dawlish! Let them out! Why, you fool, you——'

Dawlish simply lunged forward, with a speed of action and a length of reach which took the other completely by surprise. He twisted Smith's arm and the gun dropped. He pushed Smith into the room again, scooped up the gun and followed him. Smith was gasping for breath, but Dawlish appeared as calm and unconcerned as if nothing untoward had happened. Yet in fact it was as if a hurricane had swept through this place. Smith, mouth wide open, backed unsteadily into the big room.

'Do sit down,' said Dawlish, with deceptive pleasantness. He spread his great hand out, placed it on Smith's chest and pushed. Smith dropped down into the chair like a bullet. 'There's something you don't realise,' Dawlish remarked, moving towards the drinks, pouring a little more brandy into each glass. He handed Smith his, and the man was trembling so much that brandy almost spilled over the sloping side of the glass. 'I can arrest you on about a dozen counts. Attempting to bribe a police officer is one. Threatening a police officer with a gun—two. Attempted murder—well, you didn't actually shoot, so perhaps we'll skip that one. Inciting others to violence— the others being your two johnnies now in the john. Unlawfully . . . well, never mind. That's enough to be going on with. I think you will get at least ten years' imprisonment on these counts alone.'

'Dawlish! You wouldn't be such a fool! Half-a-million . . .'

'I told you, you've been trained in the wrong school. It isn't that I wouldn't like half-a-million, but I'm old-fashioned. Such words as honesty, integrity, incorruptibility, decency, loyalty, still mean what they say to me. No, your money—or Omniscience Unlimited's money won't buy me, and so won't buy you off your ten-year sentence.'

'You would never——' Smith began, but his voice had lost its positiveness.

'Oh, yes, I would,' Dawlish insisted grimly. 'You don't realise what a spot you are in. I have only to charge you. Within ten minutes policemen can be here to take you off. I would ask for a remand in custody when you appear in court tomorrow, and that's what would happen. Eight days in a remand cell at Brixton Jail. Then, committal for trial, another two or three months incarceration with all the privileges of a man awaiting trial. Finally the trial itself. After that, penal servitude, which could mean anything from breaking stones on Dartmoor to picking oakum indoors. With luck you might one day become a trusty. Did I say ten years? With remission for good conduct, you would probably be a free man again in seven. Are you married?'

Smith sank further and further back in his chair during this harangue, and when Dawlish had finished he seemed to have shrunk, and his eyes seemed huge. Halfway through he took a sip of brandy but it did not seem to help him in the slightest.

Dawlish stopped on that 'Are you married?' Smith did not

answer, simply moistened his lips. Dawlish was about to speak again when the telephone bell rang, and Smith started. Dawlish moved into a position from which he could watch the man, and lifted the receiver.

'This is Dawlish.'

'Sorry to worry you, sir. This is Detective Inspector Caution of the Flying Squad. Did you know that your apartment—in fact the whole building you live in—is being watched?'

'Yes and no,' said Dawlish. 'I just pulled a couple of men in from the landing, but——'

'I know about that, sir,' interrupted Detective Inspector Caution. 'They have been replaced by two others. And there are six altogether in the building—two in the main hall, two at the side hall, two in the garage—sorry, that makes eight. The main driveway is also covered, sir, and the building is being watched by at least another six men in three different cars.'

After a pause, in which Dawlish drew a very deep and wondering breath, Caution went on: 'I think I've spotted them all, but I can't be sure.'

'You've done remarkably well,' Dawlish managed to say.

'Thank you, sir. Do you wish me to take any action?'

'I want you to be very careful indeed,' said Dawlish. 'I'm quite sure each man is armed.'

'We could easily check by searching one man, sir.'

'No,' Dawlish decided without hesitation. 'Not yet anyhow. I'd like them all followed, individually. Better say traced—if we follow they will only lead us on a false trail.' As he spoke he saw Smith's expression changing, saw some confidence returning to the man who sat up straight, sipped his brandy and looked towards the door. 'Chief Inspector, do you know the man known as The Professor?'

'Not personally, sir, but I do by reputation.'

'Have him telephone me as soon as you can,' requested Dawlish. 'Tell him it is a very urgent matter.'

'Very good, sir. Is that all?' Caution added with a touch of humility.

'For now, yes. Where are you at this moment?'

'In my car, just outside your building.'

'Be *very* careful,' repeated Dawlish. 'This is a most peculiar situation. I——'

'Excuse me,' interrupted Caution, his voice suddenly rising. 'One of my men is attracting my attention.'

66

There were sounds of voices, muted, and then Caution came back with a note of excitement sounding clearly. 'A policeman spoke to one of the drivers in a car standing near here, sir—it was badly parked; the man didn't speak English, and neither did his passenger. They showed some resentment when they were moved on.'

'No violence?' asked Dawlish.

'Do you really *expect* violence, sir?'

'It wouldn't surprise me at all,' Dawlish told him. 'Did the man find out what language?'

'He thinks Spanish or Italian, sir, but isn't sure. Apparently the man often put a vowel at the end of his words, Italian style so to speak.'

'Your chap is a very good policeman,' Dawlish applauded. 'Get his name. And let me repeat: be very careful indeed.'

'This *is* concerned with the murder of David Kemball and Alan Crayshaw, isn't it, sir?'

'Yes.'

'Excuse me for saying so,' said Detective Inspector Caution, 'but shouldn't *you* be careful?'

'Never more so,' Dawlish assured him. 'Get me the Prof. as soon as you can.'

He rang off, looking towards the window and the lights of London in the distance, hardly realising that darkness had fallen; he had been here with Smith a long time. As his hand lingered on the telephone he saw Smith's whole body stiffen, then saw the man put a cigarette to his lips. This was the first time he had shown any interest in smoking. Dawlish, very, very intent, took a book of matches from the telephone table, struck one and leaned forward.

'Light?' he asked.

He saw Smith's cheeks pucker, and felt quite sure that the cigarette was a kind of blowpipe, that Smith had gone over to the attack.

CHAPTER TEN

THE THREAT

There was a glint in Smith's eyes and great tension in his body. Obviously he thought he had fooled Dawlish, whose face was only two or three feet away from him; at that distance no one could miss. Dawlish simply moved his head and shoulders to one side, as a boxer would move to avoid a punch. Smith gave a sharp, hissing blow of air. Something shot out of the cigarette, passing Dawlish's face with perhaps an inch to spare. Almost before he himself realised what had happened, Dawlish dealt Smith a resounding blow with the flat of his hand, and Smith keeled over. Dawlish turned, to see a tiny dart in the back of a winged armchair. It looked no more than a needle, shining in the pale light. He studied it for a moment, and saw that it was hollow, rather like the business end of a hypodermic syringe. He glanced over his shoulder and saw that Smith, recovering very quickly, was half out of his chair.

Dawlish swung towards him and Smith shrank back. Dawlish reached him and seized him by the scruff of the neck and pushed him towards the dart. Smith resisted, leaning the whole weight of his body against Dawlish's arm, but he was a pigmy in the hands of a giant, and there was nothing he could do. Yet he kept trying.

'Take it out,' Dawlish growled.

'No, no!'

'*Take it out.*'

'No, I daren't, I ...'

'Well, I dare,' Dawlish said. He took his handkerchief from his pocket, gripped the end of the needle and pulled it free. It gave a little tearing sound, and when he saw the tip there was a little piece of fluff from the chair covering attached to it. 'Fish hook type,' he remarked, roughly, and pushed Smith so hard that the man staggered a few feet and then came up against another chair. He edged behind it, as if he were in urgent need of protection. Dawlish was surprised, in a way appalled, by his own reactions. It was as if the cold-blooded killing of the two men had affected him so that he wanted to strike back on their behalf, wanted vengeance for them. His own violence, towards the blonde and the brunette, the two men in the cloakroom and now with Smith, was something which he had to control very carefully: it could soon turn from violence out of anger to violence for its own sake.

He rasped: 'Come here.'

'No! No, I . . .'

'Then I'll come to you,' Dawlish said. 'One tiny scratch on your cheek——'

'*No!*' Smith screamed. 'Don't touch me with it!'

'You meant it to stick in my cheek, so a little scratch can't hurt.'

'It will kill me!' screeched Smith.

Yes, thought Dawlish, he believed it; the man was white with fear. He carried with him a weapon of death which he would use without the slightest compunction. The temptation to go towards him, to beat him into a pulp, to beat the truth out of him, was almost overwhelming. Dawlish hardly knew how to exert his own self-control.

'What's on the tip?' he demanded.

'Cutenison,' Smith muttered.

'Instant death, in other words,' Dawlish said icily.

Smith made no attempt to deny it. He stood behind the chair ready to use it as a shield should Dawlish show any sign of tossing the dart at him. It was very still and silent in the room. Slowly, very slowly, Dawlish's rage eased. When it had gone, he knew exactly what to do, how to handle this situation. And one essential thing now that he had gone so far was to frighten Smith even more.

'You've got one chance,' he said abruptly. 'Come away from there and listen to me.' As Smith looked fearfully at the dart, he pushed it back into the chair, then draped a handkerchief over it, so that he would not sit there in a moment of forget-fulness. He watched the man return to his former position, noting his almost mechanical movements; sometimes Smith behaved like a robot, but there had been nothing of a robot in the way he had shown fear of death. 'One chance,' Dawlish repeated. 'Talk.'

'I—I can't talk.'

'Then I shall find a way to make you, or you will go to prison.'

Smith's mouth worked; his whole face seemed to twist and

distort.

'You—you don't understand.'

'What don't I understand?'

'What they will do.'

'Who are they?'

'My—my sponsors.'

'Messrs. Omniscience Unlimited?'

'It's not—not funny,' Smith muttered.

'Maybe it's funnier than you think,' said Dawlish.

The man's pallor was as great as ever, the fear was still stark within him.

'What will they do?' Dawlish demanded.

'They would never let me go to prison.'

'How would they stop you?'

'They—they would kill me.'

Dawlish thought, almost with a twinge of pity: he believes that; he is pretty sure it's true. Then he realised with a sense of shock that it probably *was* true—that Smith had no doubts at all.

'There is such a thing as police protection,' he remarked.

'It wouldn't save me.'

'I could smuggle you out of here,' said Dawlish, and realised that his very words were a concession to his own realisation that Smith's fears were justified. 'It's been done before.'

Smith closed his eyes. It was almost impossible to believe that this man who had come in with such abounding confidence, who had been so absolutely sure that he had the Deputy Assistant Commissioner in his pocket, could change so much. He sat with his head back against the chair, then began to shake his head very slowly from side to side.

'You don't understand,' he said wearily. 'You just don't understand.'

'Try me,' urged Dawlish.

'You don't know how powerful they are. They would kill me. Either as we left here or in the cell, in the Court tomorrow morning. They would kill me. Once they've put the finger on you, you haven't a chance at all. And if I were to talk ...' he shivered, opened his eyes and looked at Dawlish with piteous entreaty. 'They would know, they would find out within a few hours. There's nothing they can't find out. No Government department, no court, no bank or factory or business operation is safe from them, Dawlish. I wouldn't have a chance. No

70

one has a chance against them: There's only one way of surviving, once you've come up against them: that is by joining them.'

He spoke with utter conviction; and he looked hopelessly defeated.

Very slowly, Dawlish said: 'There is a way to beat them, Smith.'

'If you knew how powerful they were, you wouldn't say that,' Smith protested; his fear seemed to grow stronger every moment.

'There's a way to beat them,' Dawlish insisted. 'In spite of the men who surround this place, in spite of their so-called omniscience. I . . .'

For a second time, he was interrupted by the telephone, and he felt sure that this would be the Professor, whom he was so anxious to see. He moved and plucked up the receiver, rehearsing in his mind what he had to say, and announced:

'Dawlish.'

'Mr. Dawlish,' a man said in an educated and well-modulated voice, 'I wish to speak, please, to Mr. Smith.'

Dawlish was so startled that his expression must have given his reaction away, for Smith stiffened immediately with renewed alarm. The speaker had spoken very much as Smith would have done, taking it for granted that he would not be denied what he wanted.

'*What is it?*' breathed Smith.

'Are you his employer?' asked Dawlish.

'*Oh, my God!*' gasped Smith.

'I am a colleague,' the other answered. 'Be good enough to put him on the line, please.'

After a pause, Dawlish said quietly: 'I'm not sure that I want him to talk to you or to anyone.'

'Mr. Dawlish,' the man said, in exactly the way Smith had spoken earlier, 'this is not a matter for discussion. You will know by now what is wanted of you. If you are being difficult, I need to know. Put me on to Mr. Smith.'

'Mr. Smith,' said Dawlish apologetically, 'is temporarily indisposed.'

'If you have harmed . . .'

'I've simply put him to sleep for a while,' Dawlish stated, looking over the telephone to Smith. 'May I give him a message?'

There was a long pause, and in spite of himself, Dawlish could not keep back a tiny shiver, as if he were subconsciously afraid. Then the man at the other end of the telephone spoke with great deliberation.

'No, Mr. Dawlish, but I have a message for you. If you do not release Mr. Smith within the hour, and allow him to go his way unharmed, then you yourself will not live the night out. Nor will your wife.'

The speaker replaced the receiver without another word.

Dawlish put his receiver down very slowly, feeling a chill creeping into his blood. That had not been an idle threat; the speaker had meant exactly what he said. He almost certainly knew where Felicity was, and there was no shadow of doubt about his readiness to kill. Smith, still sitting there, looked as if the mark of Cain were stamped on his brow. There seemed no life, no hope in the man. And he would know the odds. Even Dawlish, so new to Omniscience Unlimited, already knew a great deal. For instance, how easily this place had been surrounded. How people sprung to do whatever 'they' ordered. He was still standing there, trying to make up his mind what to do, when the telephone bell rang again. He let it ring several times, then lifted the receiver.

'Dawlish,' he announced.

'Hallo, Major,' a man said in a bright, Cockney voice. 'Understand you got an urgent job to be done! At your service, Major, same as ever.'

'Ah,' said Dawlish with great relief. 'Thanks, Prof. I knew I could rely on you.' He hesitated. 'Hold on a minute.' His eyes closed, he appeared to be oblivious of Smith and appeared not to care how long he kept the Prof. waiting. Then he asked: 'Do you remember Ossy Parkinson?'

'Could I ever forget him!' The Prof. had a laugh in his voice at the very thought.

'Can you come and see me with someone of his build and character?'

There was a long pause; then the Prof. said: 'Character, Major?'

'Yes. As tough as they come.'

'No,' answered the Prof. 'They don't come like that any more, Major. What have you got in mind? A very sticky job?'

'Very sticky indeed,' Dawlish told him, in a tone which could have left him in no doubt.

72

There was another long pause, and during it Dawlish thought he could hear the Prof.'s heavy breathing. Then: 'Will I do, Major?'

'It's very sticky indeed,' Dawlish emphasised.

'What's life without a risk?' demanded the Prof. heartily. 'You wouldn't ask for it unless it was urgent, would you?'

'No,' Dawlish agreed, very quickly. 'How soon can you be here?'

'In about half-an-hour, I should say.'

'Bring your bag of tricks, won't you?'

'Trust me,' answered the other man. 'Never travel on business without it.'

Without giving Dawlish a chance to say another discouraging word, he rang off.

Dawlish put down the receiver, carrying a picture of a dapper man with a berry-brown face, in his mind's eye. The Prof. had worked for and with him in Intelligence during the war, and to this day was a consultant to Scotland Yard. He was a past master in the art of make-up, and in the war years had made Dawlish and others up in such a way that no one could possibly have recognised them. He had often dropped by parachute behind enemy lines to do this, and his courage was of the almost casual, matter-of-fact kind.

Dawlish was keenly aware of Smith, watching him, and as he relaxed, Smith said in a helpless voice:

'Nothing you do can save the situation, Dawlish. You've kept me here too long. You've signed your own death warrant as well as mine.' In a more spirited way he went on: 'Why the hell didn't you take the money? You could be rich—you could have pushed the stakes up to a million pounds if you'd had the sense.'

'The question is whether you have any sense,' retorted Dawlish.

'I tell you ...'

'Can you speak to the man who called you?'

'It won't do any good!'

'Can you talk to him?' demanded Dawlish.

'Yes, I but ...'

'Call him,' Dawlish said sharply. 'If you want any chance at all to live, call him. Tell him I'm holding out for more money and ask him how high you can go. Then tell him you need at least another hour, maybe two——'

Smith's eyes were opening wider.

'But——'

'Do you *want* to die?' Dawlish demanded, bleakly.

Very slowly, Smith got out of the chair and lifted the telephone. He covered the dial with one hand as he dialled with the other, to prevent Dawlish from seeing what number he was calling, but that was a trifle which didn't matter at the moment. Dawlish was aware of the ringing tone, then of Smith saying:

'Give me Jumbo, quickly—this is Smith.' There was a brief pause, and then Smith spoke again in his normal speaking voice, as if he were absolutely sure of himself. Dawlish felt a sneaking admiration for him. 'Jumbo—Smith here ... Understand you just telephoned ... Oh, don't take any notice of that, Dawlish is a great one for a joke. I was in the bathroom ... Well, I know one thing, he won't join us at the price ... Half a mill ... O.K. Well, I don't know. Can I double it? ... I tell you I don't know, he's a tough nut ... All right, I'll try three-quarters, but I'll need time ... Half-past eleven now, I can see Big Ben from here ... Well, at least an hour, maybe two ... Let's say two o'clock. You hold everything until two ... Of course I'll make it quicker if I can, but this Dawlish, he's really something ... Right ... Goodbye.'

As he spoke, Smith was smiling broadly, as if he could be seen. When he finished he put down the receiver and turned to Dawlish, and his face was like the face of death.

CHAPTER ELEVEN

THE PROF.

'IT won't save us,' Smith stated. 'You've argued too much.'

'Do you really want to save your life?'

'Like hell I do!'

'You wanted me to switch sides.'

'I offered you plenty,' Smith said bitterly.

'Now I'm offering you plenty if you'll switch,' Dawlish said. 'I'm promising you your life.'

'You could never beat——'

'Smith,' interrupted Dawlish. 'You've been under the Omniscience influence too long. They are not unbeatable and are not all powerful. When we know all their contacts in these high places, we can push them over like a stack of cards. *Be quiet!* I can offer you your life. Turn Queen's Evidence and give the police all the help you can and I think I can promise you freedom as well as your life. If you're so sure this great Omniscience will kill——'

'Don't keep using that bloody word!' screeched Smith.

Dawlish said quietly: 'All right, Smith. And will you play?'

Smith sat back again and closed his eyes. Once again the room was very quiet. Outside two men were doubtless waiting, and near by there was the concentration of men watching both of them. How was it that such an organisation existed without the police knowing? If the police anywhere had any knowledge of this, then it would have filtered through to him by now. He poured out more brandy, but Smith waved it away. He went to the passage, glancing back when Smith must have thought he was out of sight. The man sat there, obviously deep in harrowing thought. Cautiously Dawlish opened the door of the cloakroom, remembering that these men might be armed with the killer-darts, or with knives, but realising one or the other might be badly hurt. Both had regained consciousness. Before they realised that the door was open he slammed it on them again and turned the key.

Dawlish went back to Smith.

The emissary had moved from his chair to the window and was looking out over the wonderful panorama of London, seeing the reddish glow in the sky which denoted Piccadilly Circus and the pale floodlight which swept St. Paul's.

There seemed no rebellion in Smith now; no threat. Without turning round, he asked: 'Can you promise me I'll go free?'

'No. But I think we could get you a Queen's Pardon, if it even reaches that stage. There's no guarantee,' Dawlish said.

'But you'd try?'

'I'd pull every string I could.'

'What—what do you want me to do?' asked Smith, moistening his lips.

'First. I've a man coming here to take your place,' Dawlish told him. 'He's a make-up artist, and he'll leave here looking exactly like you. You'll need to tell him where to go, what to do.'

'The trick would be spotted in a few seconds,' protested Smith.

'How far do you have to go to report?' asked Dawlish.

'As—as far as Marble Arch!'

'That's not very far, but——'

'Once the masquerader stepped inside Bell Court——' began Smith, only to break off as if in horror at the realisation that, unwittingly, he had given something away. It seemed to Dawlish that he was beginning to break up; that the unexpected and almost immovable opposition had broken his morale and his will power. There might be something else; he might have realised even before arriving here, that his time was running out, that sooner or later he would come to the end of the game. Whatever the reason he was a changed man, and Dawlish had no doubt as to the genuineness of the change. The fear in Smith's eyes was too real for doubt.

'Well, what would happen once he stepped inside?' asked Dawlish.

'He would need to know the code, the password. He would have to report, there isn't anyone in this world who could disguise himself well enough to get away with it.'

Dawlish said thoughtfully: 'No, I think you're right.'

'Then the whole situation is hopeless!'

'Not if you think it right through,' Dawlish said. 'Once you are away from here,' he paused and then asked as if a new idea had occurred to him: 'How did you come?'

'By car.'

'Did you drive yourself?'

'Yes. I've a red Ford Cortina, parked outside. But——'

Dawlish interrupted: 'If my man took the car and drove towards Marble Arch, what would happen? Would your Jumbo or whoever is in command call off his dogs?'

'Dogs?' asked Smith blankly.

'Watchers,' explained Dawlish.

'Oh. Oh, yes,' answered Smith. 'They are here simply to make sure I'm not arrested or kidnapped. They would disperse as soon as I appeared. One or possibly two of them would follow me to Bell Court.' He gave a funny little laugh and threw up his hands. 'You see, I've lost control already. I keep naming the place.' Despite the words a gleam of hope

76

shone in his eyes. 'I still don't understand you.'

'If my man—the Prof. short for Professor—leaves here looking like you and heads for Bell Court, he can take his time, and then he can run for it,' said Dawlish. 'I'd back him against anyone in the world to shake off his pursuers. And while he's being mistaken for you, we can take you to a nice quiet spot where you'll never be found, and where you can talk your head off.' Dawlish gave a sudden broad grin. 'You haven't any choice about what we do—and you'll be a bloody fool if you don't talk freely. It's the one hope you have of a future.'

Smith didn't answer; he looked like a man who had lost all hope.

Fifteen minutes later, the Prof. arrived.

He was a little taller than Smith but very similar in build, and when they switched clothes, Smith's fitted the Prof. almost as if tailor-made for him. He had a merry twinkle in his bright blue eyes, his pleasant, nondescript face sunburned to a deep tan. As Dawlish told him what was wanted, he was assessing Smith's face with wholly professional interest. Smith hardly said a word.

'Okay, I can fix it,' declared the Prof. with absolute confidence. 'Use your bathroom, Major? ... Great one. the Major,' he added earnestly to Smith. 'Why, during the war ... my gosh, what a lot of muck they put on your face ... where's that spirit gum softener? ... got it ... Dropped behind enemy lines more times than anyone else alive, the Major ... Absolute inspiration he was, to hundreds of us ... there was a time—put your head on one side, chum—when he dropped straight into a P.O.W. camp, you know, Prisoner of War camp—and made off with a Colonel who had to be got out of that camp somehow ... Ruddy marvel ...'

Dawlish could hear the almost unceasing rumble of the voice as he telephoned his office, talked with the Night Duty Supertintendent and arranged for Smith to be taken to a Security House, which was in fact a nursing home in Hampstead. The police made arrangements like clockwork, and quite suddenly Dawlish, a lone wolf by preference, was aware of the other side of the coin and the advantages of team work.

Almost as he finished, the Prof. called: 'Spare a minute, Major?'

He went into the bathroom, prepared for what he was going to see—yet absolutely astonished. For two men, as like as two peas, stood looking at him.

'Prof.,' he declared, 'you're a genius!'

'My mother always said I was,' remarked the Prof. complacently.

'If we've got another twenty minutes, Major, how about making *him* look like me as I really am? Fool 'em proper that would!'

Dawlish stared for a few moments—and then gave a little, almost light-hearted chuckle.

'No need to make him look like you,' Dawlish said. 'Provided he doesn't look like he does now.'

'Oh, I'll make a new man of him,' declared the Prof. and Smith actually gave another weak laugh.

Half-an-hour later, both men were ready to leave. Smith looked much older than when he had arrived, and grey. While the Prof. had padded his shoulders and wound a sheet about his waist so that he was much plumper. Dawlish did not think there was the slightest chance of either being recognised as themselves, but the important factor was whether the Prof. would be taken for Smith.

'Never doubt it,' the Prof. said heartily. 'Not for a minute.'

But Dawlish knew, and the Prof. must have known, that he was going out to what might prove his death ... And there was nothing Dawlish could do but wait at the telephone as reports came through, with Smith at an extension, as desperately anxious to know the results as Dawlish himself.

Soon one of Caution's sergeants was on the radio telephone and in direct contact with Dawlish. And the reports about the Prof.'s movements began to come in.

'He is at the lift, sir.'

'He is in the main lobby.'

'He is walking towards the red Cortina—the only one in the driveway, sir.'

'He's getting in.'

'He's starting the engine.'

Dawlish felt himself go hot and cold, and saw the sweat on Smith's forehead.

'He's backing out, sir.'

'He's going out on to the Embankment ...'

'He's being followed by two men in a Morris 1100 ... sir ...'

Dawlish moistened his lips, and his grip on the telephone was very tight.

78

The Prof.'s grip on the steering wheel of the small car was quite loose, and he looked wholly relaxed, although there could be no doubt about the danger or the odds. Dawlish had made it very clear, and Smith's manner must have emphasised it. A Morris 1100 pulled out from the driveway behind him, but neither slackened nor quickened its pace. He had been briefed on the route which Smith himself would have taken— Parliament Square, St. James's Park, The Mall towards Buckingham Palace, then Hyde Park Corner, Park Lane—inside Hyde Park going north—Marble Arch and then along the Bayswater Road. Bell Court was a new high rise building on a big site between the Bayswater and Edgware Roads, only recently opened, and known to be expensive and luxurious. On a traffic-free night the drive wouldn't take much more than ten minutes, but with traffic one would take at least half-an-hour. As he turned into Parliament Square, a little sports car swung in front of him. He had plenty of clearance, but pretended not to have. He jammed on his brakes, the car jolted to a standstill, the Morris 1100 stopped only inches away from his rear bumper.

His engine stalled.

He kept his foot right down, flooding the carburettor, and kept pulling at the self-starter, getting only a grating noise. The sports car vanished, snorting, along Queen Victoria Street. The Prof., muttering under his breath, saw the driver of the car behind getting out—then saw a policeman heading towards him. The driver got back and the Prof. wound down his window.

'Having trouble?' the policeman asked, face at the window.

'That ruddy sports car ...'

'Yes, I saw it, but you were doing a fair turn of speed yourself,' the policeman remarked flatly.

'Now look here ...'

'It's okay,' the policeman interrupted. 'I'm not going to charge you.' He gave a boyish grin. 'Think you can get her started?'

'Well, one thing's certain, mate. I can't stay here all night.'

'You never said a truer word,' said the policeman.

The Professor looked at him startled, saw his grin, realised that he had probably been alerted by the C.I.D. and tried the engine again. The Morris 1100 was still behind.

'Do something for me,' asked the Prof.

'What?'

'Move those baskets behind me—they make me nervous.'

'Anyone who could make you nervous deserves a medal,' the policeman retorted. '*Can* you start?'

'Gimme a few more minutes.'

The grating sound of the self-starter sounded very loud and clear on the quiet night. The policeman, directing traffic round the two cars, spoke to the driver of the Morris 1100, then pointed. With obvious reluctance the driver moved off. The engine turned, suddenly, and as it did so, several cars came out of the Courtyard of the House of Commons; then there came a stream of them, the House had risen, tired M.P.s were anxious to get away. More policemen appeared to control the sudden rush of traffic, and the Prof. wasted several more minutes, waiting for a chance to slip into the stream of cars. When at last he moved, he found the Morris 1100 double parked opposite the Downing Street steps. He went past and was followed.

So far there did not appear to be the slightest suspicion. He had gained—or lost—ten minutes, and there was no need to worry about time. At Hyde Park Corner, however, there was almost rush hour traffic as one or two big functions ended. Park Lane was clear and he sped along it, then swung left at the approach to Marble Arch, and left again.

Now, he was close to Bell Court. He could see the lights in its higher windows, a floodlit pillar. There was a wide carriageway in front of it, and only a few cars were parked there. He turned in, still followed, but the Morris 1100 passed along the street as he turned into the carriageway. A doorman stepped towards him, hand outstretched to open the door.

The Prof. stopped. The door opened.

'Like me to put her away, sir?'

'Yes. I—Oh damn!' exclaimed Prof. in a fair imitation of Smith's voice. 'I've forgotten something. Won't be long.' He leaned across and slammed his door, and started off again. The doorman moved back, almost off his balance. The Prof., as if elated, crowed: 'I've done it!' and then as he swung out of the carriageway he saw another car move towards him, obviously intent on a broadside-on crash. He jammed his foot on the accelerator, and shot forward, felt his bumper catch and the car shudder. There was a sound of metal on metal and then he was free. In his driving mirror, he saw the other driver recover and knew there was pursuit. Then he saw another car, at the end of this street, which led to the Edgware Road. And he saw a man level a gun. He ducked. A bullet smashed the glass at the side window and pieces flew, stinging but not cutting him. There was another bullet, which struck the side of the car, before the Prof. reached the corner and swung left, towards Maida Vale and away from the heart of London.

The other car followed, and he set his teeth as he drove on.

'Two shots have been fired,' the sergeant told Dawlish over the radio telephone. 'They're heading up the Edgware Road.' Then the man's voice shrilled with excitement. 'It's all right, sir! One of our cars has pulled in front of the pursuing car, got it for speeding, I bet. *Your* man's away, sir!'

'Thank God for that!' exclaimed Dawlish, and for the first time since he had come home, he felt that he could relax, but he did not think he would be able to for long. He went into the bedroom and began to undress, and almost at once, the telephone bell rang.

'Dawlish,' he announced.

'Smith's safely in the nursing home,' a man reported. 'He seems to have collapsed, and the doctor says he has taken some kind of morphia sedatives—put himself to sleep for several hours.'

I should have expected it, Dawlish thought, but he had not, and there was no point in blaming himself. In any case, he needed sleep; and he would be much more able to cross-examine the man in the morning.

'Well, we'll have to let Smith sleep until I come.' He gave a gargantuan yawn, smothered a laugh and said: 'What about the other two chaps you took from here?'

'Spanish speaking, sir, that's all I could find out,' the other answered.

'We'll know more in the morning,' Dawlish said: 'Good night.' He set the alarm clock for seven o'clock which allowed him five hours' sleep, and slept like a log.

CHAPTER TWELVE

BREAKFAST

By a quarter-past seven Dawlish was up and shaved, thirsty because he hadn't allowed himself time to make tea. He went out at half-past seven, into an empty hall and landing, but there were two men from the C.I.D. and one from his own department in the main foyer, as well as the night doorman. His own man, youthful-looking, balding with a flat nose, went out with him to his car.

'Will you drive?'

'No, I want to talk on the telephone.' Dawlish settled into his seat and picked up the telephone. 'You know where we're going, don't you?'

'Home Office.'

'That's right.' He lifted the telephone and called his own office, through *Information* at the Yard. Childs answered, almost at once.

'Hallo—couldn't you sleep?' Dawlish asked.

'Good morning, sir,' said Childs, and went on in a tone of reproach: 'I learned what was going on.'

'Do you know what happened during the night?'

'The Prof. is safely home,' Childs told him. 'Incidentally what about payment for him?'

'A hundred guineas should be enough. What about the two prisoners?'

'Spanish speaking and believed to be Puerto Rican or Argentinian,' Childs answered. 'We tried a number of interpreters but only the Spanish got any response. They understand it, but won't talk. They're obviously imported thugs.' That was strong language for Childs.

'What about the man who fired at the Prof?' asked Dawlish.

'He wasn't caught—they're all pretty slippery customers. There were a dozen watching your place but when the man they thought was Smith was brought out of the building, they simply drove off. And although some were followed, they all got away.'

'And the men who chased the Prof.?' inquired Dawlish.

'Charged with speeding,' answered Childs. 'No one quite

knew what you wanted done, so we all played safe.'

'Good enough. And I didn't really know what I wanted myself. Any report from Security?'

'The man who calls himself Smith has come round,' Childs said.

'I want you to see him,' Dawlish decided. 'Tell him his only chance of safety is to tell us everything he knows. Go in with a tape-recorder, and use your own initiative on what to do. If he gives any trouble I'll have a go. What about Bell Court?'

'It's being kept under surveillance,' answered Childs. 'Mostly from rooftops and windows of neighbouring buildings. We have a continual patrol of plainclothes men passing.'

'Keep it that way, I want you to watch all comings and goings,' ordered Dawlish. He felt the car slowing down as he went on: 'It looks as if I've reached the Home Office. I'll come straight to you when I'm through.'

'I hope you have a very good breakfast, sir,' said Childs.

The doormen in uniform at the Ministry had obviously been alerted to expect Dawlish, and one of them came forward to open the car door as he drew up.

'Mr. Deputy Assistant Commissioner Dawlish, sir?'

'Yes.'

'We've just been told that the Minister is expecting you, sir. Please come this way. We will look after the driver and the car.'

There was a huge lift; an atmosphere of peaceful quiet; wide corridors; an indication, almost, of palatial opulence. He walked on a thick, figured carpet until eventually they arrived at a big, mahogany door. The doorman tapped, the door was opened by a middle-aged man.

'Good morning, sir.'

'Good morning. How many others know I'm here?' inquired Dawlish.

'I gave instructions at seven o'clock this morning, sir—that is customary. This way, please.'

It was like a scene in a film, and Dawlish found it difficult not to laugh. The most pleasant and ordinary of politicians were, once in office, surrounded by this near pomp and cere-mony. They went across a thickly carpeted room past a very large and important desk, past leather tomes behind glass, un-til a door facing them opened and Montgomery Bell appeared. He was in his shirt sleeves and without a collar.

'The Deputy Assistant Commissioner for Crime, sir, Mr. Patrick Dawlish.'

'Ah, yes. Do come in, Mr. Dawlish.' Bell stretched out his hand. He was taller than Dawlish had remembered, hook-nosed, with a thrusting chin and well-shaped lips. His eyes were dark and heavy lidded. 'All right, Simms.' He closed the door on the older man as Dawlish stepped into a small room, with a dining table, a side-board with a hot plate, coffee bubbling in a percolator, a toaster standing by. 'I always like to make my own toast and coffee if my wife isn't about to make it for me—she's in Scotland for a few weeks. Do sit down. Oh, and help yourself.' He lifted a big silver plated cover off a dish of bacon and eggs. 'Tea, if you'd prefer it,' Bell went on. 'I won't be a jiffy.'

'Coffee will be fine, thanks.' Dawlish was helping himself when Bell reappeared, this time with the tie and jacket in place.

'A trencherman, I see,' he remarked with approval. 'Personally, I was always a substantial breakfast eater. Like all condemned men!'

Dawlish carried his laden plate to the table as Bell put bread into the toaster.

'Condemned to what?'

'Politics! The responsibility of being part of the Government,' Bell explained, and added lightly: 'Did you know that Cabinet Ministers have a shorter life than bishops?'

'It doesn't surprise me. Minister...'

'Shall we be a little less formal, Dawlish?' Bell sat down, his own plate laden, coffee and bread and toaster all within hand's reach. This man was a natural organiser, in small things as well as large.

'Good idea,' said Dawlish. 'I was going to say, I think I made a lot of progress during the night.'

'Ah, good.'

'But I'm not sure you will like much of what I found out,' went on Dawlish.

'Try me,' said Bell. He began to eat, then went on with a kind of growl in his voice: 'Don't take too much notice of me, Dawlish. I am trying to cheer myself up. The whole situation is most depressing. After I talked to you last night, I was with some of my colleagues—some in and some on the fringe of the Cabinet. We are all deeply troubled.'

'About the passport business?' asked Dawlish.

'That, and so much more. Dawlish . . .' Bell paused to drink coffee, and to butter toast. The everyday actions seemed to give added vehemence to his words: 'We seem to have lost all privacy.'

'Ah,' said Dawlish.

'Cabinet decisions—recommendations from permanent civil servants to the Government, policy proposals—they all seem to be known almost before they're made,' said Bell, and he seemed angry as well as troubled.

'Yes,' said Dawlish.

'You sound almost smug,' said Bell, tartly. 'Don't tell me you know this.'

'I was told about it last night,' Dawlish answered.

'You were told——' Bell broke off, obviously in astonishment.

'I had a visitor who offered me half-a-million pounds to work with a group which I called Omniscience Unlimited,' explained Dawlish. 'I'm pretty sure they took it for granted I had a price. When they realised that I hadn't, they were badly thrown. If they want to buy someone in any position of authority or influence, or if they want to buy informers or lower-echelon help, they simply find the man and then his price. And they've learned that it nearly always works.'

'Good God!' Bell gulped down toast as if it hurt. 'And what did you do to your chap?'

'Sent him packing,' Dawlish said airily.

'But Dawlish! You could have held him!'

'Yes, couldn't I,' said Dawlish drily.

'What—my God! What *did* you do? How——'

'I don't propose to tell you,' said Dawlish, very simply.

'You don't *what*?' Obviously Bell could not believe his ears. He had stopped trying, or pretending, to eat, and glared across the table, while Dawlish ate with the single-minded concentration of which he was capable whenever food was at hand. 'Dawlish, I hope you realise what you are saying. You are a senior police official. I am virtually the second-in-command of home affairs. That includes all police business. I am so infinitely senior to you that I can order your instant dismissal.'

Dawlish neatly dissected a sausage.

'Stop this nonsense,' he said flatly, and lifted a laden fork to his mouth.

'My God! I *will* have you dismissed!'

'For being loyal?' suggested Dawlish mildly.

'For deliberately defying an instruction.'

'For being honest, refusing to accept the odd half-million or so bribe so that these people could put me in their pocket, too.'

'Dawlish.' The Minister pushed his chair back and stood up. 'I want to know what action you have taken and propose to take about the man you claimed visited you and made this incredible offer.'

'Oh, he meant it. And did I tell you his name was Smith? His employers must make quite a profit, mustn't they?'

'Dawlish, I shall inform the Prime Minister of your astonishing behaviour.'

'Do,' urged Dawlish amiably. 'You might also care to tell him that my visitor knew last night that I was going to have breakfast with you here this morning.' He buttered a small square of toast. 'As you called me on a private line you presumably did not want even your secretary to know about the arrangement at that time, so who do you think could have told Mr. Smith?' Dawlish poured himself out more coffee, but eyed Bell very straightly. 'Who but you could have told him, Bell?'

Bell stood up, glaring, hands clenched.

'Well—who else could have?' demanded Dawlish.

'You—you can't be serious!'

'I am deadly serious,' insisted Dawlish. 'Either you told him, or someone in your department and in your confidence did. I wouldn't dream of confiding in you about my plans for Mr. Smith. I don't think it would be a safe risk.'

'Safe,' echoed Bell. Suddenly he moved back to his chair and dropped into it. He seemed to have aged years in the past few minutes, but Dawlish had not turned a hair. There was silence for several minutes, until Bell said:

'I am not a traitor.'

'Then you have a traitor in your confidence.'

'I can't believe that.'

'You must believe it. Are you a wealthy man?' asked Dawlish sharply.

'No. I——' Bell began, and then stopped abruptly.

'Very bribable, and so very corruptible,' Dawlish said. 'Tell me one thing, sir. Are you being blackmailed?'

Bell did not answer at once, but pushed his chair back

again. His whole body was a-tremble, and he did not seem able to find words. They were staring at each other when there was a low-pitched buzz, and, startled, Bell glanced at the door. Then he pressed something beneath the table, and said: 'What is it?'

'You asked me to remind you when it was eight-fifteen,' a man said through some kind of microphone. 'You are to see Sir Gerald Knighton at eight forty-five.'

'I—er—yes. Simms! Just a minute,' said Bell, huskily. 'I—my business with Mr. Dawlish will take longer than expected. Ask Sir Gerald to come at *nine* forty-five instead.'

'But sir! Mr. Arbulhart is due at . . .'

'Put all my appointments back by an hour,' ordered Bell.

'But you have to see the Prime Minister at twelve noon,' the unseen man sounded horrified.

'Make what adjustments you think are necessary in order to make that possible,' ordered Bell. 'Cancel one or more of the appointments if necessary. Is that clear?'

In a subdued voice, the man answered: 'Very good, sir.'

Bell pressed the push under the table again, leaned back, closed his eyes and spoke without opening them. 'I have a reputation of never being late for an appointment and never cancelling one. That is why I am always so early starting in the morning.' He opened his eyes: 'Dawlish—I am not a traitor.'

'But you *are* being blackmailed,' Dawlish remarked, sounding as deeply disturbed as he felt.

'Attempts have been—are being—made to blackmail me. Yes.'

'On what grounds?' asked Dawlish.

'That is surely——' Bell began, and then he saw Dawlish's expression harden. He paused, and said sharply: 'An indiscretion which any wife would not approve.'

Dawlish looked away.

'How many other of today's leading politicians have been involved in this way, I wonder. Tell me, are there photographs?'

'Yes.'

'Do you have one here?'

'I have a print, but——'

'May I see it?' asked Dawlish.

After a few moments of hesitation, Bell said: 'I don't really see why I should allow you to bully me in this way.'

'You don't have to,' said Dawlish. 'And I don't mean to be overbearing. I'm suffering from very great pressures, you know. If you're right, and the man Smith is right, then this nation is in very grave trouble. May I see that print, please?'

Bell opened a drawer in the desk, and then pressed one side, revealing a skilfully concealed partition. He picked up a credit-card type of holder, and from between two stamp-sized cards he withdrew a small, square print. He held it out.

Dawlish looked at it. If he was shocked at the nudity and posture of Bell and the blonde, he hid that well. It was the fact that the blonde was the same girl who had lain unclothed on his own bed the night before which sharpened his interest.

CHAPTER THIRTEEN

HOW WIDESPREAD?

They sat there for a long time, and the only sound was the bubbling of the coffee pot. When Bell could bear the suspense no longer, and while Dawlish stood looking down, he burst out: 'Well! Do you know her?'

'I spanked her last night,' said Dawlish quietly.

'You—*spanked* her? Good God!'

'And I threw her out of my flat and threatened to have her arrested for indecent behaviour or exposure or whatever would be the correct charge. She didn't take the risk. How—ah —long ago did this particular rendezvous with her take place?'

Bell looked him straight in the eye, as if he could no longer face evasion. 'Three weeks and a day——' he broke off, help-lessly. 'Well, I needed some relaxation.'

'You appear to have got it,' Dawlish remarked drily. 'When did they start putting pressure on you?'

'They've asked for trifles of information but didn't really get going until two days ago,' Bell answered miserably.

'And presumably you were then told to find out how much I'd discovered and pass it on to them.'

Bell said stiffly: 'Dawlish, what they wanted me to do and what I would have done aren't necessarily the same things.'

'Did you tell them I was coming for breakfast?'

'Yes.'

'Then why the devil did Smith let me know they knew?' marvelled Dawlish aloud. Almost immediately he went on: 'To impress me with their omniscience, I suppose. They were very anxious to impress me, but why should they be, when they've half the Government in their pocket?'

Bell was still looking at him very straightly and with a kind of offended dignity. 'I think that is an exaggeration, Dawlish. A grave exaggeration.'

'I hope so,' Dawlish said gruffly. 'I certainly hope it is. Have you any idea how many of your colleagues are under the influence, as it were?'

'No,' muttered Bell. 'I've no knowledge.'

'Two—four—six—eight——' Dawlish began.

'Certainly three or four,' interrupted Bell glumly.

'What is the general feeling of the victims?'

'Despair,' answered Bell, and gave a deep sigh. 'Absolute despair. They get on with their job as well as they can. It's like living in a nightmare, Dawlish. Part of the time it seems bearable, at others, utterly intolerable.'

'That's reasonable enough,' Dawlish said with understanding. 'Do you mean despair because each is himself involved and faces some kind of disgrace or scandal?'

Bell said heavily: 'Well, there's that of course. I certainly wouldn't want to have that picture spread across a front page. But I don't think that is the main reason. It—it's much more —patriotic. Much less selfish than that. We feel that this thing has got so far that there is nothing we can do to stop it. Vital economic and military secrets as well as political and industrial secrets have already been given away. Some members of the Government, those whom I know are involved, feel that they are helpless. And we also suspect that most Cabinet Ministers as well as Junior Ministers are under pressure and won't yet admit it. We know the stranglehold is widespread but don't know how widespread, yet.'

'I see,' said Dawlish. 'Are you prepared to try to find out? To give me the names and addresses of everyone involved?'

After a long pause, Bell said frankly: 'No. I am not prepared to gamble with you. You may not realise it but you are only a cog in the machine, Dawlish. So am I. I dare not risk jamming the machine at this stage. If I tell anyone it will be the Prime Minister, not you.'

After a long pause, Dawlish asked quietly: 'Do you know what is being planned? What the stakes are?'

'No,' repeated Bell. 'I was simply told to find out what you knew.' For the first time since the conflict had arisen between them, he smiled faintly. 'You didn't intend to let me know, did you?'

'No,' said Dawlish.

'Do you really know anything that matters?'

Dawlish studied him closely, and then said: 'Nearly enough to smash them, I think. Better not tell them so, though.'

Bell sat down very slowly. Almost automatically he poured himself another cup of coffee. 'You wouldn't tell me a thing you didn't want to be passed on, would you?'

'Right in one,' said Dawlish. 'When you're asked, I want you to be in a position to tell them a great deal. For instance, that I have Smith; that he is being interrogated and is talking freely, which means that I know as much as he does. And you could tell them that I am the only man who stands between them and disaster. They wanted me badly enough before, but nothing like as desperately as they want me now.'

'I don't understand,' said Bell. 'Surely, if they think you are in their way, they will simply kill you.'

'Then they'd bring about their own disaster,' Dawlish said. 'If they were to kill me, everything I know would be broadcast to the world. And it's quite a bit.' In fact, it was desperately little, but he spoke with all the assurance at his command, knowing that this would be passed on to Jumbo.

Jumbo! The incongruity of names! What could sound less sinister than Jumbo? 'While I'm alive, I might keep my knowledge to myself.' He gave a sudden, deep laugh. 'I might even be bribable!' He pushed his chair back and went on: 'That was a very good breakfast. Thank you.'

'Dawlish, what can I say to the Prime Minister?' Bell demanded. 'He was as anxious about this meeting as I was.'

'Tell him,' said Dawlish earnestly, 'that I have the matter well in mind, I am leaving no stone unturned, no avenue unexplored, to resolve it satisfactorily. If I go on as pontifically as that,' he added even more earnestly, 'I shall qualify for a high political post, won't I?'

He started for the door, and Bell hurried to open it for him.

'This—this has been absolutely confidential, hasn't it?' Bell urged, deep pleading in his manner.

'I shan't breathe a word to a soul,' promised Dawlish. 'Unless I happen to meet that blonde, of course.' Then he stopped, towering over Bell, and his voice hard and grating. 'But get a list of Cabinet Ministers and others whom you know are involved. I want that in exchange for keeping quiet about you.' He went out, stoney-faced, led by the watchful Simms through the labyrinth of passages.

As the door closed on him, the Rt. Hon. Montgomery Bell, M.P., Secretary for Home Affairs, drew a hand across his forehead, and dropped into a chair. He was trembling; his teeth actually chattered. After a few minutes his pallor lessened. He put his hands beneath the table, fumbled for a few moments and at last pulled off a tiny tape-recorder. He placed this on the table, and pressed a switch in it. There was a whirring sound as the tape rewound, then a click, then his own voice sounded and eventually, Dawlish's. He wiped his forehead again, stopped the recording and put the tiny instrument in his pocket.

'Now I wonder if I said anything I didn't want passed on,' Dawlish asked himself as he went down the steps of the Home Office. His driver stood at the open door of the car. 'No thanks,' he said aloud. 'I'll walk. I need some fresh air.'

'It certainly is a beautiful morning, sir.'

And indeed it was. The sun shone warmly on Dawlish's fair hair and broad shoulders, as he strode along Whitehall, thinking about several things at the same time. He felt sure he was being followed, and that had to be expected. He felt equally sure that the danger was very acute. He contemplated the ugly fact that he could trust no one. With a matter of such magnitude, one dare not trust even those one supposed to be trustworthy. The knowledge of his loneliness in this savage and crucial affair was heavy on his heart. Yet it *was* a glorious morning, with the spires of the towers of the Horse Guards vivid in the sunlight, and, as he neared Parliament Square, the tower of Big Ben and the Gothic splendours of the Houses of Parliament acquired an almost fairy-tale beauty, as if they were pictures in the mind rather than actual buildings which housed the hopes of so many people.

Including his own ...

He turned into the little street leading to old New Scotland

Yard and nodded to a constable on duty, walked up the dark, near-deserted marble-like hall and reached the lift, then his own office. As he entered from one door, Childs entered from the other.

'Hallo,' Dawlish said, and added heavily: 'Problems?'

'Very grave ones I think,' said Childs, simply.

'An ultimatum?' inquired Dawlish, 'from the Smith seniors?'

'Yes, sir.'

'Tell me,' said Dawlish resignedly.

'There have been four telephone calls,' Childs told him. 'Each was from a different man, or else a man speaking in a different voice. The name given was always the same.'

'Jumbo, by any chance?' asked Dawlish.

'I do wish you'd told me more, sir.' Childs was still reproachful. 'Yes—Jumbo.'

'I don't know but I imagine that's a blanket name for certain echelons in Omniscience Unlimited—which is my phrase,' he added hastily. 'They seem to know so much and they think they know all. Were there any threats?'

'Yes, sir. Unless you allow Smith to go free they threaten to——'

'(a) Kill me,' interrupted Dawlish. '(b) Kill or kidnap my wife. (c) Disgrace and discredit me for ever in the eyes of the world. (d)...' he paused in turn, frowning. 'I don't quite know what they would threaten for (d). Tell me.'

'There was no fourth threat,' Childs replied equably. 'The fourth message was of a different nature. If you release Smith and co-operate with his superiors, the tax free sum you can rely on receiving is one million pounds, and in addition a tax free income of fifty thousand pounds a year.'

'Oh,' Dawlish said, stroking the broken ridge of his nose. 'Quite a lot of money. What was offered you as an inducement to persuade me to agree?'

'Ten per cent of the amount promised to you,' Childs answered, without batting an eye.

'Ah. Also quite a sum of money. You could retire in comfort, couldn't you?'

'I could indeed.' Childs was standing in front of the desk. He had much more impressive dignity than Bell, and there was an impression of pride in his fine grey eyes. It was a strange thing, thought Dawlish, that he had always taken

Childs for granted. His efficiency, his knowledge, his remarkable memory, his knowledge of world affairs, world personalities and people, world crime, criminals and policemen. Only in the past few months had Dawlish began to see him as a man reaching the age of retirement; a tiring human-being who had worn himself out in the service of his country. Only today had Dawlish really noticed the depth of lines about his eyes and at his mouth. All of these things flashed through Dawlish's mind as Childs went on with slow deliberation: 'Will you answer a question, sir—a question of great personal importance to me?'

'Yes, of course,' said Dawlish.

Childs drew in a deep breath. 'It is very simple, Mr. Dawlish. Do you trust me?'

It would have been so easy to say quickly, even glibly, and with ninety-nine per cent of truth: 'Yes, of course I do.' But Dawlish, returning Childs's gaze with one of great frankness, didn't give that answer at once. When at last he spoke, his words held grave deliberation.

'Until this morning, I trusted you absolutely,' he said.

'Did you last night, sir?' Childs asked. 'You withheld a lot of information from me then, you know. You knew that I was standing by. Normally you would have talked to me freely, but you didn't.'

'No,' Dawlish admitted. 'I didn't.'

'Why not, if you trusted me?'

It was a strange situation; virtually another conflict, and Dawlish sensed how important it was. This man, whom he had so taken for granted, had great strength of character and stubbornness and, in his moment, steely defiance. Dawlish could not be sure what was going on in his mind; was not even sure that he knew what was going on in his own. In a way, too, the relationship between them had changed. In a quiet, unobtrusive manner, Childs had taken the initiative. But Dawlish welcomed the questions, because they enabled him to analyse his own reactions and so to see the situation more clearly.

'Probably several reasons,' he answered at last. 'I was extraordinarily tired ...'

'You gave instructions for action to someone else, sir.'

For the first time, Dawlish felt a flash of annoyance; and it must have shown in his face for Childs seemed to stiffen. But personal pique was not important at such a juncture, and it might dangerously distort judgment, so he went on evenly:

'Yes, of course I did. There was no need to disturb you with my anxieties. I have trusted you always, but I've also been aware that you are getting older and that you need more rest than you used to. I wouldn't disturb you when you were off duty unless it were for something only you could do.'

He paused, for Childs to say:

'Thank you. I do understand your consideration.'

'As for why I didn't talk to you about what was going on, that's easy,' Dawlish said. 'I had a quite positive and pressing need to think over everything that had happened and digest it all, trying to see its full significance. I didn't want to talk to you or anybody, only to leave everything in the think-box and see what came out in the morning.'

'Your subconscious thinking is quite remarkable,' Childs murmured, and then added in a barbed quietness, 'And on this occasion, it told you to distrust me.'

'Not directly,' Dawlish said. 'It told me to trust no one. I have just come from the Minister for Home Affairs. In this particular case I wouldn't trust him an inch. I know for a fact that he had a tape-recorder fastened beneath his breakfast table—I touched it. And I suspect it was for the Omniscients.' Dawlish gave a grim smile. 'It could have been for himself or for the Cabinet, but I doubt it. On my way here I was going over everything I said and wondering whether I'd put my foot in it anywhere,' Dawlish added. 'You see, I don't even trust myself.'

'We aren't talking about that kind of trust,' said Childs. 'Were you satisfied that you had said only what you would want the—ah—Omniscients—to know?'

'Yes,' answered Dawlish. 'I'm sure they believe that I have a lot of information, and I've encouraged them to think so. I'm sure they fear I could break them wide open, and everything I said confirmed that. But no one, not even you, knows how much I have discovered.'

'I see, sir,' Childs said into a pause.

'Childs,' Dawlish went on. 'I don't trust the staff at the Home Office, I don't feel I should trust anyone. Something has happened in political affairs which I don't understand. It looks as if there has been a kind of infiltration inside high Government offices, business houses and industrial companies.

'I haven't yet seen or fully understood all the implications. One wrong move, and there could be disaster. I would rather offend, affront, humiliate and hurt you than take the slightest chance. I'm not going to take that chance. In my position, would you?'

Again Childs moved back from the desk, but his expression had changed slightly, he looked—was mollified the word? And he actually smiled as he answered:

'No, sir. I would not.'

'I didn't think you would.'

'On the other hand, sir, in your position—and even if I had your enormous strength of mind and character, your—your Atlas-like propensity to take the whole world on your shoulders, if I may put it like that, I would still feel that I must confide in someone. I would not be able to carry such responsibility alone. Can *you*, sir?'

The smile remained on the pale lips and lurked in the grey eyes. With it, there was a direct challenge. Childs was compelling Dawlish to face up to the situation in every way; was even saying, with remarkable directness, that it was wrong for him to take too much on his shoulders. And it would be.

But, at this moment, before he had been able to absorb and fully understand what was going on, was it safe to confide in a living soul? No one could be sure how much he knew—or how little he knew. Wasn't this a 'game' which he must play absolutely on his own, at least for a while?

CHAPTER FOURTEEN

DISAPPEARANCE

Childs seemed to fade into the far distance. Dawlish was facing the situation in his own mind, and was not influenced by this man or any other person. There was truth in his inclination to take too much on his own shoulders; to feel that there were some jobs which only he could do. But—there were such jobs, and he felt quite sure that this was one of them. He sat there for a very long time, with these reflections passing through his mind, before he came out of what must have seemed a trance, and spoke quite crisply.

'Not for long,' he said. 'I hope for long enough. And there are some things we have to trust each other about, anyhow.'

'I trust you, sir. Implicitly.'

'Thank you,' Dawlish said almost humbly. 'I believe you do. Thank you, Jim. Now! What news are we getting from abroad, about the passports?'

'Nothing reassuring,' answered Childs promptly.

'Is the massive passport fraud world-wide, then?'

'It's rampant in the United States, Canada, Australia, New Zealand, India and Pakistan and in many of the new African nations, as well as most of Europe,' answered Childs. 'There is some trouble in Eastern Germany and Russia but their *visa* system makes it more difficult. But as things are, a great number of people have passports which really belong to other people. The two men we arrested do have genuine Argentinian passports but they are duplicates. The most virulent criminals can move about freely with such passports.'

'What details have we?' Dawlish wanted to know.

'Hardly any,' answered Childs, and then amended: 'Well, very few. Labollier feels we should convene a conference very quickly, preferably in Paris,' he added, smiling faintly.

Dawlish didn't answer.

'Did you hear me, sir?'

'Yes,' answered Dawlish slowly. 'I heard. Jim—if we're in our present plight at Government level, other countries may be, too.'

'Yes, obviously,' observed Childs.

'And so other police forces may have been infiltrated,' Dawlish went on.

'Also obviously possible,' Childs agreed.

'And so the Crime Haters may have been infiltrated,' Dawlish said in a very gentle voice.

'It's hard to believe but it *could* have happened,' agreed Childs painfully.

'We couldn't feel the complete confidence we have always felt in the delegates, not even in those men whom we have known for a long time. That doesn't necessarily mean that it would be unwise to call a meeting, though.'

'No,' agreed Dawlish slowly. 'It could cut two ways.' He stood up and began to pace the office, frowning at the ceiling. Suddenly one of the telephones on his desk gave a slight buzz. A pale blue light showed that this was a call from outside the department and the Yard, and it was to his private number.

'Did Jumbo call on this line?' he demanded, left hand out-stretched.

'Yes,' said Childs.

So there's a leakage here, thought Dawlish and plucked up the receiver. 'Dawlish speaking.'

A man spoke very quickly. He had a low-pitched, pleasant voice, his English was good, but there was some kind of accent which told Dawlish that he wasn't English born.

'Good morning, Mr. Dawlish,' he said. 'I imagine that you have had our message by now.'

Dawlish looked up at Childs, and waved: Childs went swiftly to his own office where he would listen on the extension. The door opened and closed as Dawlish said in a slightly-over-hearty manner:

'Mr. Jumbo, I presume.'

'You presume correctly, Mr. Dawlish. And before we go on I would like to make one thing absolutely clear: You person-ally, and your wife, and indeed your nation, are in very grave danger. None of our threats is idle, and we have all the facili-ties for carrying them out. Don't have the slightest doubt about that. That, incidentally, is why such highly placed poli-ticians as Mr. Bell will not give you information. I repeat——'

'I've no doubt at all,' Dawlish interrupted.

'Then you will release Mr. Smith.'

'Not yet,' said Dawlish pleasantly, 'I need a much longer talk with him first. And I would like to have a talk with you before I come to any decision.'

'You may not talk with me or with anyone in authority in this organisation until Mr. Smith has been released,' stated the man who called himself Jumbo.

'A great pity,' said Dawlish, 'and a somewhat arbitrary con-dition. Goodbye.'

He replaced the receiver and smiled vaguely at the map of the world through which he could get into almost instant touch with any delegate of the Crime Haters at any time. At the back of his mind there was awareness of some undefined factor that was badly wrong, but sooner or later he would be able to place it. Meanwhile he must keep thinking, must stay calm. A sense of panic was not far away.

His telephone from the New Scotland Yard rang, and he lifted it quickly. 'Dawlish.'

'Good morning, sir. This is Chief Superintendent Lancaster.' It was almost a relief to hear a man who was about his everyday duty.

'Hallo, Lancaster,' Dawlish said. 'How are things with you?'

'I've got a bit of something new,' Lancaster announced, with obvious satisfaction. 'Mr. Kemball was having quite an affair, apparently. Until late last night I'd come to believe that after his second wife's death he was a bit monastic, if you know what I mean—but apparently he went out twice a week to see a friend, during which time the neighbour, Mrs. Halkin, looked after Kathy. Often Kemball wasn't back until nearly one o'clock. Interesting, isn't it?'

'Very interesting indeed. Have you traced the woman friend yet?'

'Not yet, but it shouldn't take long.'

'Get cracking, will you?' Dawlish asked. 'The need for urgency in this case couldn't be greater.'

'We won't lose a moment,' Lancaster promised. 'Don't worry, sir.'

Dawlish put down the receiver but had hardly had a moment to ponder before the door opened to admit Childs. Almost at once the outside telephone bell rang again. Dawlish put his hand on it and said to Childs:

'Check that my wife's all right, will you?'

'She rang just before you came in, sir. I promised you'd ring back.'

'Thanks.' Dawlish lifted the receiver, and announced:

'Dawlish.' He was thinking that he should give much more thought to Felicity, and must make sure that Beresford's place was impregnable.

'Good morning, sir.' This was Detective Inspector Caution who had taken Smith away. 'Caution here. I'm at the Security place now, sir.'

'Yes.'

'There's a long message on the tape-recorder we put in last night, but Smith won't give it to me. He says it's for you, and no one else.'

'Reasonable enough in the circumstances,' conceded Dawlish. 'How is he?'

'I think he's all right—a bit scared, that's all. He had a pretty big breakfast anyhow.'

'Good. Tell him I'll get over as soon as I can,' promised

Dawlish, and rang off.

Childs was staring down at him, and Dawlish told him the gist of what Caution had said. Childs nodded understanding and Dawlish went on with a touch of bitterness in his voice:

'I haven't taken enough precautions at Hampstead.'

'I have, sir.' Childs was almost smugly reassuring. 'I felt that Mrs. Dawlish and her friends should have absolute priority, so the house and whole neighbourhood is full of our men and Yard and Divisional men. All tradespeople are checked as they go in, too. Mr. Beresford hasn't left for the city yet; he asked for a word with you before he goes.'

'That's wonderful,' Dawlish said, adding: 'Thanks, Jim. That will teach me not to trust you! Get Beresford for me. If the man calling himself Jumbo comes through while I'm talking, let me know. I don't want to make him bad-tempered for the sake of it.'

Childs nodded, and went into his own office. Almost at once, the call to Ted Beresford's house came through, and Ted himself was soon on the line.

'Ted!' exclaimed Dawlish.

'Do I detect certain signs of extra anxiety in you this morning?' Beresford asked. 'This place is absolutely swarming with what I hope are coppers.'

'They are,' Dawlish assured him. 'There could be an attempt to kill or kidnap Felicity.'

After a moment's silence, Beresford observed:

'Bit like the old days, Pat. Pretty big stuff, eh?'

'Very big stuff,' agreed Dawlish, simply.

'Think I should stay home today?'

'Can you?' asked Dawlish.

He was puzzled by the lengthening pause which followed. Normally Beresford, who was a senior partner in his firm of stockbrokers, would have said 'Yes' in his deep drawl and somehow a sense of enthusiasm for staying at the house would make itself evident. Now, however, he was obviously filled with doubts. At last, he said:

'Yes, I can. But should I? Pat—supposing I go now and get back early.'

'Why not stay?' asked Dawlish, more puzzled than ever.

'Somehow I think I should be on the spot myself this morning,' Beresford said. 'I don't feel that I can really trust anybody these days. To get a job done properly one has to do it oneself. And I know that one of the smaller banks we work with have some pretty tricky problems. If I'm not there my chaps might panic, and panic would bring the shares tumbling.'

'Good God!' exclaimed Dawlish.

'Something bitten you?' demanded Beresford, sounding almost nettled. 'If you're thinking that my banking customers should come second to Joan and Felicity I agree, but...'

'Not that at all,' Dawlish said with sharp conviction. 'Can we lunch somewhere today?'

'Glad to. Where?'

'Let's say here,' suggested Dawlish. 'Is one o'clock all right for you?'

'I'll be through by then, thanks.' Beresford paused, and then went on: 'Pat—you *do* feel sure that everything will be all right, don't you?'

'Yes,' Dawlish said. 'Nothing will go wrong in the next few hours. Let me have a word with Fel, will you?'

'She has just gone into the garden with the children and the dogs,' Beresford said. 'Hold on.'

Dawlish held on.

At first, he was not perturbed, because obviously it would be a few minutes before Felicity could reach the telephone. In the first short period of waiting, he was as calm and light-hearted as he had been for a long time. He had a picture of Kathy Kemball in his mind's eye, at the window of the bungalow; and now he was able to picture her as she played with the Beresford children and the Beresfords' two cocker spaniels. A new life was opening for her, and somehow he had to help make that life good. Childs came in with the tele-typed reports from some overseas countries. The one from Australia was particularly disturbing—they had 'lost' over three thousand passport numbers. At the foot of this message was a personal note from the Sydney, New South Wales delegate to the Crime Haters.

'Shouldn't we soon have a big pow-wow, Pat!'

'We'd have enough of a problem with the passports alone,' said Dawlish. 'Anything else in?'

'A note about Alan Crayshaw,' said Childs. 'Can I hold on for you?'

'No, thanks, my wife will be on the line at any moment. Don't say Crayshaw was having a love-life too.'

'He was marital fidelity itself,' answered Childs. 'But his bank statement shows one or two heavy credits in the past six months, final confirmation that he was bought. The two prisoners taken at Clapham simply won't say a word. They are almost certainly Spanish speaking, like many of the men who appear to be employed by the—ah—Omniscients.'

He turned and went back to his office.

Dawlish thought: 'Could we have been cut off?' and then he heard sounds at the telephone and his fears quietened. This would be Felicity, picking up the instrument. He actually smiled in anticipation, and was startled to hear Ted Beresford's voice. It sounded like the voice of doom.

'Pat, she's gone,' he said. 'Fel's gone.'

Dawlish echoed stupidly: 'Gone? Where?'

'Pat, she's—she's disappeared.'

Dawlish thought, in a strangely calm and detached way: He is saying that Felicity has disappeared. He couldn't speak for that moment, he felt so choked, and Beresford went on:

'The children are all there. A play ball disappeared in the shrubbery. Pat—we're searching the grounds, but I'm afraid she's vanished absolutely.'

This was no illusion, no hoax, no mistake. Beresford was too solid and reliable a man to say all this if there was the slightest doubt. In spite of the police 'swarming' about the neighbourhood, the garden and the grounds, Felicity had been kidnapped. Dawlish could almost hear the voice of the Jumbo who had telephoned him.

'Mrs. Dawlish,' a man had said to Felicity.

'Yes?' Felicity said. 'Just a moment.'

She retrieved a rubber ball from a shrub in which it had become lodged, tossed it back to the children, saw one of the spaniels race towards it as it rolled along the grass, saw Kathy also racing towards it, her face radiant. Felicity had time to reflect on the miracle that a few hours and a sound night's sleep could bring, and on the easy forgetfulness of a child. Then she turned back to the man.

'I'm Chief Inspector Worthy, madam.'

'Oh, I've heard my husband speak of you,' said Felicity.

'Good things, I hope,' the man said almost coyly.

Felicity did not greatly take to him. He was big and broad, his face rather a hard one. But she was able to say truthfully:

'Very good things.'

'Glad to hear it.' Her affirmation was received with a faint smile. 'Your husband's up the road in a closed car, Mrs. Dawlish. He would very much like a word with you but doesn't want to be recognised by anyone else—it's a quick visit, ma'am.'

'Oh, I'll come,' said Felicity. She did not give a thought to the possibility of danger, and was all eagerness to see Pat. The children and the dogs were happily absorbed in each other, and would not need her for the next few minutes or so.

She said pleasantly: 'Isn't it a lovely morning?'

'You've said it. We could do with a nice week or two.' The man gave her a hand up the steep bank, along the top of which ran the road. Half-a-dozen men were in sight near the closed gate. Pat certainly wasn't taking the slightest chance with her or the child. 'There's the car, Mrs. Dawlish.'

It was a big, rather efficient Daimler, reflective of the old-worldiness of some Government departments. A peak-capped chauffeur sat at the wheel. Felicity was a little surprised that he wasn't standing by to open the door.

'Pat——' she called.

Suddenly she was lifted off the ground and pushed into the car, a thick cloth thrown over her head and shoulders. One moment she had been full of eager expectation, the next she was filled by a wave of terror. She pitched forward, helplessly and painfully. A man gripped her wrist and twisted. Pain screamed through her, and she gasped.

'Quiet,' the man said harshly. 'Quiet or I shall kill you.'

As he spoke the door slammed, and the car moved slowly and sedately off.

CHAPTER FIFTEEN

THE CHOICE

Dawlish said harshly into the telephone, 'Who is the police officer in charge, Ted?'

'Seems to me to be a Superintendent Gorley, but there's a Chief Inspector Worthy, whom I met for a few moments this morning.'

'He's in my department,' Dawlish said. 'Bring one or the other of them to the phone, will you?'

'Yes, right away. I've already alerted them.'

'It would be as well to get the children indoors.'

'Right. Hold on.' Beresford's receiver clattered on a table, while Dawlish, in his office, stared blankly ahead of him, his heart cold as ice. He rang for Childs, who stopped as if appalled on the threshold.

'What's wrong, sir?'

'My wife's gone,' Dawlish said starkly. 'If the man Jumbo calls, put him through at once.'

'I will indeed. Oh, and Mr. Dawlish . . .'

A man at the other end of the line said: 'Mr. Dawlish?' It was Chief Inspector Worthy, whom Dawlish knew as a big, unimaginative, thorough and wholly reliable officer. 'I'm very sorry about this, sir.'

'Yes, I've no doubt. What have you done?' demanded Dawlish.

'Three unidentified cars were seen in the neighbourhood, sir, and I've had descriptions of all three sent to *Information*. Of course a local search was instituted at once. Mr. Gorley is looking after that. Have you any special instructions?'

'Find her,' insisted Dawlish.

'If it's humanly possible we will.'

'Find her,' ordered Dawlish in a hard voice. 'And find out who let her go.'

'*Let* her go, sir? I assure you . . .'

'You had instructions to watch every move she made,' Dawlish rasped. 'Either you or someone else fell down on the job.'

'I'm terribly sorry, sir,' muttered Worthy. 'Terribly sorry.'

'Find her,' ordered Dawlish, and he rang off.

There was Childs, at the communicating door, and there was a mental picture of Felicity hovering above Childs's head, and a picture of big, reliable Worthy. Reliable? Dawlish stared for what seemed a long time, and then barked:

'Well?'

'Jumbo is on the line,' announced Childs, quietly.

Dawlish nodded, and picked up the telephone. He did not hurry to reply, nor did he take too long. He had to maintain his self-control; somehow, he had to keep calm. There were a dozen ways Dawlish could have spoken, from rage to cold, calculating hardness, and the one he chose—it was as if some instinct chose it for him—was mild and untroubled. He lifted the private telephone.

'So you're back,' he said, with obvious satisfaction. 'I thought you wouldn't be long. Where shall we meet?'

'We are not going to meet anywhere until Smith has been released,' said the man who had spoken to him before. 'And I want him released at once, or——'

'You are simply wasting your time,' Dawlish interrupted.

'Or your wife will be killed,' stated the man called Jumbo.

Dawlish's heart contracted and he clenched his teeth, but those things passed, and when he spoke again it was as calmly as if he had not heard.

'Smith stays with me.'

'Dawlish! Did you hear me?'

'Of course I heard you.'

'Your *wife* is in acute danger,' Jumbo repeated with great vehemence. 'All you have to do so as to free her is to let Smith go. I am *not* making an idle threat. Your wife's life——'

'Is in my hands, I know,' interrupted Dawlish. Then he added more briskly: 'No deal, Jumbo.'

Faintly, the man said: 'But your wife!'

Dawlish put down the receiver without another word. But he was sweating freely, his whole body seemed clammy and the hand with which he had held the receiver was sticky and warm. Like a jack-in-the-box, Childs appeared again; he would have heard everything on the extension, of course. Dawlish was aware of him but took no notice. He was utterly motionless; and he felt as if his blood had turned to ice.

Childs, listening on the extension, could hardly believe his ears. He had known Dawlish in all manner of moods and all manner of crisis, but had never known him behave in this way. As he heard the receiver go down he had rushed to the door; but Dawlish's expression seemed to mesmerise him.

Dawlish was sitting like a graven image. Something in his expression, or the nerves of his face, had tightened so that his bones seemed to be more prominent and his cheeks thin. His eyes seemed more deep-set too, as if they had been carved out of some hard, dark metal. Childs did not feel that he could speak; nor did he feel that he could leave his chief alone in such a mood and at such a time. Dawlish appeared to be quite unaware of him as he moved to a corner cupboard, took out brandy and a glass, poured out a little and carried it to the

104

desk.

'Drink this, sir.'

Dawlish started, and looked at him.

'What?'

'Brandy, sir. Please drink it.'

Very slightly Dawlish seemed to relax, but there remained something almost terrifying in his expression. He took the glass, after a long pause, opened his mouth and tossed the brandy down. It made no apparent impression on him.

'Well?' he said. 'Ever gambled with your wife's life?'

Childs said: 'He won't harm Mrs. Dawlish, sir.'

'We shall soon find out.'

'He's so used to getting his own way,' Childs went on. 'None of them seem to know what it is to be defied or thwarted.'

'How well do you know him?'

Childs caught his breath, and then said very quickly: 'You know, sir, even in these circumstances that wasn't fair.'

Dawlish stared; his jaw and forehead seemed so taut that it seemed the skin would crack. Then he gave a grotesque mockery of a smile.

'No, it wasn't,' he agreed. 'I'm sorry.'

'Thank you, sir.' Childs went on quickly: 'All the evidence is that the man is so used to riding roughshod over opposition that he really doesn't know how to take it when he runs into a brick wall. I'm sure you'll hear from him. He is undoubtedly afraid of you.'

'Not so afraid as I am of him,' Dawlish said. He looked at the telephone, and then moved his hands, the knuckles tautly white, without even a tinge of colour. Even the atmosphere seemed diffused with emotion, surging, suppressed. Then the telephone bell rang.

Dawlish drew in a deep shuddering breath. His right hand shot out towards the instrument and he actually touched it, then drew back and motioned to Childs.

'Answer,' he said.

Childs thought: He doesn't want to seem anxious. He lifted the telephone and tried to speak in a detached voice.

'This is Deputy Commissioner Dawlish's office——'

Dawlish thought: It might not be Jumbo. He saw Childs's face, and then the slight nod. So the man from Omniscience Unlimited had not lost much time. Thank God, thank God! Unless—unless Felicity had already been injured. Injured; or killed. There was such a possibility. He pictured Kemball's slashed throat—oh God, what had he done?

'Hold on, please.' Childs handed him the receiver. 'It is the man known as Jumbo, sir.'

'Thanks.' Dawlish wiped the sweat off his forehead with his free hand, and forced brightness into his voice. 'Hallo, there. Have you had second thoughts?'

The man who called himself Jumbo spoke with very great deliberation, as if he wanted to make sure that every syllable he uttered was clearly understood. 'Do you realise that you are placing your wife in jeopardy by your stubbornness, Mr. Dawlish?'

Dawlish felt a surge of relief at the 'you are placing your wife in jeopardy'. Obviously they had not harmed Felicity so far, and surely if they had held their hand for so long, then they would continue to do so: they needed to bargain as much as he needed time, and Felicity was probably the best hostage they could have.

'I know exactly what I am doing,' Dawlish said, as precisely as Jumbo.

'I'm surprised to hear it,' Jumbo said. 'I will exchange your wife, alive, for Smith alive.'

'I can't do that,' Dawlish said. 'You should know that it simply isn't possible.'

'If you don't, you will have your wife's death on your conscience for the rest of your life,' Jumbo said in a tone not far from exasperation.

'My conscience remains my affair,' Dawlish retorted. 'I want to see and talk to you. If you don't make an appointment, quickly, I shall tell the world exactly what's going on.'

'You can't *know* what's going on!'

'I know a lot more than Smith appears to,' said Dawlish. 'Unless he's being very cagey, and only telling me part of what he knows.' When there was no immediate answer, he said, 'I will be at the new restaurant in Hyde Park at half-past three this afternoon. I shall be alone. If I don't get back to my office by half-past five, then everything will be broadcast. If I were you I'd come alone—not with your bodyguards.' He paused, long enough for the man to respond, but there was no answer. 'Goodbye,' he said, and rang off.

As the telephone went ting! he wiped his forehead again, but now there was a certain calmness, as of a position accepted, and action decided.

'Do you think he will come?' Childs asked.

'Yes,' Dawlish said. 'Yes, I do.' But he couldn't be sure, there was no way of being sure; and the realisation tormented him.

'*Do* you know enough to——' began Childs, then broke off and gave a twisted smile. 'You won't tell me, will you?'

'Not yet,' said Dawlish. 'I think everyone would be surprised at how much I do know!' For a moment he sounded almost gay. 'I've a lot to do between now and half-past three, including lunch, here, with Mr. Beresford. And—how many big businessmen and bankers do we know?'

Childs said, startled: 'Quite a number.'

'Well, I'd like to talk to a few of them. Get Mr. Maxwell of Scotland Yard on the telephone, will you? Oh, and some hot coffee.' He was already dialling a number. 'I'll talk to Sir Alfred Factor at the City of London Police ... Hallo. Sir Alfred, please ... Dawlish ... Deputy Assistant Commissioner ... Alf, how are you? Oh, alive, you know. Alf, I'm told that there are some disquieting rumours about leakage of information in the city ... Stock and share leaks, advance information about balance of payments, the gold reserve and ... There are? How long have these things been going on?'

He listened intently for several minutes, and then added: 'Thank you ... I'll call back later, and meanwhile if there could be a list of these things with a separate list for any leakages to do with foreign currencies and investments I would be very grateful. Thanks.' He rang off, and without a pause plucked up the other telephone. 'Chief Superintendent Maxwell? ... Hallo, Max, sorry if I kept you ... I've just been talking to Sir Alfred Factor. He tells me there is a great deal of disquiet in the city because of leakages of information about movements of bullion and pre-trading Stock Exchange activities ... You deal with much the same kind of business here with a greater emphasis on commercial activity, don't you? ... Do you find the same situation there? A general disquiet? ...'

Again, he listened very intently, and then he said: 'Thank you very much ... Yes, there are some indications of this in overseas investments and trading, too. I'm trying to find the source. If you could supply a list, with a separate one for any overseas trading, I would be ... You will? I am most grateful. Goodbye.' He rang off, and stood up, went to Childs's door, opened it and asked: 'Did you get all that?'

'I did indeed,' Childs said.

'Good. I'm going out,' went on Dawlish, going in and picking up one of two cups of coffee on a table by Childs's side. 'I'll be back by one o'clock for Mr. Beresford.' He glanced at his watch, and saw that it was a little after ten o'clock. 'At least I've some time in hand.'

'Yes,' said Childs. 'Is there anywhere I can get you?'

With only the slightest of hesitation, Dawlish said: 'I'm not sure where I'll be.' He knew that Childs took that as another deliberate refusal to confide in him, but this was no time to study Childs's feeling; and this was a matter of great importance.

He was going to see the man Smith at Security.

The awful part, reflected Dawlish as he drove along a narrow street in Fulham, was that he really could not trust anybody, not even top people in security. He might be making a terrific mistake but for the time being he knew that he had to do everything for himself. Now, in a rented car, he drove towards the place known at the Yard as Security.

This was in fact a row of small houses in a short street in Fulham, not far from the Thames. Across the wide river, beyond the enormous traffic roundabout at the new approach to Wandsworth Bridge, was Wandsworth and one of the more commercial parts of London. Here, in Fulham, Security was at the entrance to a papermaking factory, and many of the little terraced houses near by belonged to the factory and were occupied by the workers. Most people in the vicinity took it for granted that the particular terrace where Dawlish stopped was privately owned.

In fact, it was maintained by the police for certain prisoners on remand who had to be segregated from others and not put in the remand prisons. It was used to keep certain accused persons after their arrest—men and women who might be attacked if they were held in a police cell. Occasionally, witnesses were held here, nearly always with their assent. As far as Dawlish knew, no one outside the Yard realised what this particular row of houses was for.

There were fifteen in all. Each could be entered by its own front or back door; and although many of the residents didn't realise it, each could be entered by way of its neighbour on either side. Most of these communicating doors were cleverly

108

disguised. Dawlish had been told earlier that Smith was in Number 13, and he drew up further along the street and parked the car, then looked up and down.

No one appeared to be showing the slightest interest. He went to the front door of Number 13 and rang the bell. Almost immediately he saw a cover on a peep-hole move; he was being inspected. A moment later the door opened and he was admitted by a lean-faced young man, who said:

'Good morning, sir. I know you, of course, but may I see your card?'

'Is everything all right with Smith?' Dawlish asked, as he took his police card from his breast pocket.

'Perfectly all right,' the young man answered. 'He's restive, that's all. And he still won't let go of the tape-recorder.'

Dawlish put his card away.

'Check that I wasn't followed, will you?'

'There is a constant watch, sir. You will be informed if there is the slightest indication that you were followed or we are being watched.' He led the way up a flight of narrow stairs, then along a passage to a closed door. He unlocked it, and stood aside. Dawlish stepped into the room—and received a shock so devastating, so savage, that he felt as if he had been hurled bodily against a wall of granite.

Smith lay back in an easy chair—dead.

His throat was slashed, exactly as David Kemball's had been. The blood was still bright crimson, he had been killed recently, and here, in this security block. He must have been killed by a man who had no right here yet whom the police had allowed to get in, *or* by a policeman.

CHAPTER SIXTEEN

THE MESSAGE

Dawlish stood there, appalled.

Yet as he stood, part of his mind worked and the sixth-sense which had served him so well throughout life, served him again. He was aware of a movement behind him, and he back-heeled with terrific speed and force. There was a shrill gasp of pain. He spun round. The young man who had admitted him was backing away, face distorted, one foot off the ground. Dawlish grabbed him by the coat lapels.

'Did you kill him?' he growled. '*Did you?*'

The man's mouth was wide open, Dawlish could see way back to his shiny larynx, but only incoherent sounds came out.

'*Did you kill him?*'

Then he saw the spots of blood on the back of his captive's hand, and he had no doubt at all. Someone was coming along the passage. Dawlish pushed the young man against the wall and held him there as he ran through his clothes. As a lean, lithe, middle-aged officer appeared in the doorway, Dawlish drew a small tape-recorder from one pocket.

'What the devil——' the newcomer began and then he saw Smith. 'My God!' he gulped. 'Mr. Dawlish!'

'Yes. Who are you?'

'Detective Inspector Caution, sir. I was coming to check——' He broke off, looking at the young man. 'Tom,' he groaned. 'Not *you*.'

The young man suddenly sprang to life, snatched a knife from his pocket and slashed at Dawlish's wrist. The bloodied blade caught his forearm with a sharp pain but did no serious harm. The man lifted the blade again, and slashed at Caution in an effort to get away. Caution, with great bravery, grabbed his arm, and they stood for a moment locked together. Savagely, Tom brought his knee up to Caution's groin, but at the same time Dawlish chopped him on the back of the neck with the side of his hand. He choked, and fell.

Caution stood gasping.

'I can't believe——' he began, and then he stopped.

'You can believe he killed Smith, let me in and was ready to kill me,' Dawlish said roughly.

Pallid-faced, Caution looked straight into Dawlish's eyes. 'That's the trouble these days,' he said hoarsely. 'You can't trust anybody.'

'Trust yourself,' Dawlish said, in an equally hoarse voice. 'Charge this man with murder, and make sure he's lodged in a police-station cell under treble-guard.'

'I'll do that all right,' Caution promised. 'But I've known him——' he broke off again, and shrugged his shoulders helplessly.

Dawlish placed the tape-recorder into his inside breast pocket, and stepped towards the door of the Security block. Security! He felt the warm flow of blood on his arm, where the cut was bleeding. Awkwardly he tied a handkerchief about it, and moved towards the front door. A uniformed man, on duty, stared at the blood-soaked handkerchief, then up at Dawlish's face.

'Are you all right, sir?'

'Yes, thanks,' Dawlish said. 'Open the door for me, and keep it open in case I have to dodge back in a hurry.'

'Right, sir.' The policeman opened the door.

Dawlish stepped out on to the porch, far too massive to be hidden completely. No one was in his direct line of vision. He peered cautiously in each direction, but only two women, each wheeling a pram, were in sight. He nodded to the policeman and went into the street. There was a curious snap of finality behind him in the closing of the door.

He reached his old car, and looked inside, leaned in and released the bonnet and checked, in case of a booby-trap. There was none. He took the wheel, watching carefully in the driving mirror. No one turned into the street. He drove off, going through a maze of side streets, until eventually he was in Wandsworth Bridge Road, confident that he hadn't been followed. He turned into another side street of larger houses, drew in and sat back. Waves of shock swept over him, his wrist throbbed, his head throbbed. He rested it against the side of the car and closed his eyes. Pain seemed to be passing through his whole body. He did not know how long he sat there, but slowly he began to feel better. There was a tautness across his forehead still, but he felt he could trust himself to drive with safety.

Once or twice as he headed towards the Embankment, near World's End, he was seized by a fit of shivering, which took possession of his whole body, and time and time again he saw a mental picture of David Kemball, with his throat slashed.

And Smith——

He had been responsible for Smith's safety.

He reached the old New Scotland Yard, leaving his car at the steps for a man to park; the man stared at him with obvious curiosity, but forbore to ask questions. Dawlish went up to his office and this time the other office did not open. He looked at the cupboard where he kept the brandy, then shook his head, and rang for Childs.

The door opened almost immediately, and Childs came in. 'I didn't realise you were back,' he said, and then caught his breath. 'Mrs. D——'

'All right as far as I know,' Dawlish interrupted. 'But . . .' he told Childs what had happened, but did not tell him that he had brought back the tape-recorder. 'Make all the necessary reports and check that the murderer is on a charge, will you? Then leave me for at least half-an-hour. In fact, I don't want to be disturbed until Mr. Beresford is here.'

'I'll keep everything away from you,' Childs promised, and went out.

Dawlish got up very slowly and locked first the passage door then the communicating door. As slowly he went back to his desk and placed the tape-recorder on it. It was exactly the same model as the one he had seen at Bell's. He switched on, pressed the tiny knob for the spool rewind, then switched on the playback. As he heard Smith's voice, he seemed to see the man's face.

Gradually, his thoughts were drawn away from the murder, as he listened. For Smith, having decided to co-operate, talked with what seemed to be absolute freedom.

'I want you to understand, Mr. Dawlish, that in my opinion you have no chance whatsoever to overcome the forces which oppose you. I do not believe that what I am about to tell you will be sufficient help. However, you have already surprised me in several ways, and possibly you will again. My only hope of living is that you will succeed, so I will say all I can.

'I am a senior member of an international organisation which you have called Omniscience Unlimited. It is known to us who serve it as The Authority. I know all—well, most—of its officials at my own and lower level, but only one man, known as Jumbo, on a higher level. He is a kind of composite person. "Jumbo" is the word for his rank or authority, not his individual name. I get my instructions from him.

'I have worked for The Authority for eleven years, being tempted at first by a substantial money offer. At that time I was in the Ministry of Foreign Affairs and had access to confidential information which I sold. This put me in The Authority's power. I am a highly efficient administrator and was quick to rise in the organisation.

'The Authority,' Smith's voice went on, 'has one purpose: to obtain secret and confidential information and to exploit it at a profit. It has—so far as I know and I believe I would know if it were otherwise—no actual political aims or motivation, it simply wants control so as to extort money. It is interested in power only for the profit to be gained from it. This profit is enormous. I have seen provisional statements of accounts which show that the global income of The Authority is as great as that which Great Britain accrues from all sources.

'The Authority gains information about political and economic decisions, gold reserves, currency changes. It is the organisation which has for many years set the dollar against sterling, sterling against the franc. It operates its own international bank and has been an effective influence on the Swiss, German and American bankers who have decided what loans should be made to Great Britain, France and other nations, and on what terms. It is a major influencing power behind most, perhaps *all*, major industrial and commercial takeovers. It has reached the stage where it can manipulate Governments as easily as it can manipulate stocks and shares. And it has operated from the beginning—or from my first knowledge of it—by corrupting officials, politicians and all those who hold positions of trust, in every strata of society.

'Recently, a number of national and international police forces—including yours—have been pressing investigations into activities which are in fact controlled by The Authority. In some cases, The Authority's local power has been threatened or reduced. For this reason it has decided to take over virtual control of national and international police forces, and you of course are a key figure in the British and the main international organisation. It is believed that with your help it will be possible to learn *all* the measures so far taken by the police against The Authority, and against The Authority's national activities. This is why such a high premium has been put on your services. I can also tell you that one of the weaknesses in The Authority has been the difficulty of moving certain personnel from country to country; it has been necessary in many cases to use assumed names. This is why there has been a "take over" of certain Passport Offices. It is also why David Kemball was removed. He had discovered one way in which these passports were being used, largely through one of our lower echelon operatives, who cashed in on the side with an insurance fraud. This man, of course, is now dead, for he made it possible for Kemball to discover much more about The Authority's activity. Kemball, left alive, would almost certainly have come to you. So, he had to be killed.' There was a long pause, and Dawlish began to wonder if he had heard all there was to hear, when Smith started again.

'I can tell you no more, Mr. Dawlish, but I can give you some advice. The Authority would go to at least ten million pounds for your co-operation. They need you. If I were you, I would join them. The only other way you can stay free from them will be by death.'

The voice stopped; but it seemed to go on and on in Dawlish's mind. The story was so deliberate, the telling so restrained, that he did not doubt any of its truth. But there were no names, only a general discourse; almost as if Smith's main purpose had been to unnerve Dawlish. However, it explained what had happened so concisely that everything fell into place, from the murder of David Kemball to the murder of Mr. Smith.

And now he had only one hope of getting results: through Jumbo.

He put the tape-recorder away, and moved about the office, studying the world maps, seeing even more vividly how vital the police network was. And The Authority was right; he *was* in a position to learn of every action taken by the police everywhere; he could be vital to the success of all they were trying to do.

Ten-million-pounds...

He gave a funny little laugh, because the amount was almost beyond his comprehension. He had never been wealthy, but had always had enough money with which to live in comfort. But *ten-million-pounds*...

A buzzer sounded on his desk, breaking his reverie. He waited for it to be repeated, then lifted a receiver. 'Yes, Jim?'

'Mr. Beresford is here, sir,' announced Childs. 'And luncheon is ready in the conference room. Mr. Beresford is in there.'

'Thanks,' said Dawlish. 'Give me two minutes and I'll be with him.'

Beresford was a huge man, bigger even than Dawlish, and there were no closer friends than these two. In one of the cases Dawlish had worked on, years before, Beresford had lost a leg, yet few people, seeing him walk, would have dreamed that one leg was artificial. He had big, rugged features and the clearest and most honest-looking grey eyes, but Dawlish dared not confide in him today, could only talk in generalities, learn Beresford's story, and ask him to find out as much as he could about leakages of information in his own firm and on the Stock Exchange.

'I can do that all right,' Beresford said. 'And I'll report daily. But Pat——'

'Yes, Ted?'

'Can't I really *help*?'

Dawlish answered very quietly, very honestly: 'Not yet, I'm afraid.'

'Not even to find Felicity?'

'Not even that,' said Dawlish. 'I'll have to see this through. But look after things at home. Watch Kathy Kemball as if she were your own.'

'Be sure of that,' promised Beresford. Then, after a pause he went on: 'I've never seen you look as you're looking now. It's as if you think you can see the end of the world coming.'

'And that's about how I feel,' Dawlish replied.

When Beresford left, a little after two o'clock, Dawlish spent five very bad minutes brooding over Felicity. At last he managed to push this aside, and went through all the routine work on the desk, including the latest reports on the Kemball and Crayshaw murders. The Smith murderer had been charged and was at Bow Street police station; *he would be safe there, if he were to be safe anywhere.* Several more of the delegates to the Crime Haters Conference suggested a meeting very soon. He could not even be sure that these men were now trustworthy; they might be calling for such a meeting because The Authority was prompting them.

At three o'clock he rang for Childs.

'I'm going over to Hyde Park,' he said. 'If I'm not back by half-past five, or haven't sent a message, go and see the Commissioner at New Scotland Yard and tell him all you know. And . . .'

Dawlish took the tape-recorder out and handed it to his assistant. 'Give him that. It's Smith's statement.'

Childs looked at him steadily. 'Thank you very much.'

Dawlish gave him a bleak smile, and left the office.

The day was more than carrying out its early promise. The

high sun was bright and warm and yet not too hot. There was a pleasant breeze, but not the slightest chill. London looked at its best, and most of the people in Whitehall and Parliament Square appeared to be relaxed. Traffic was thick but no one seemed to be in a great hurry. He turned towards St. James's Park and walked across the grass. The sun had brought out thousands of people most of them elderly, or mothers with young children. The ducks of the pond strutted about or swam, glutted with food thrown by tiny hands. The tulips were at their colourful best with antirrhinums and phlox making glory against the smooth surface of the water and the recently mown grass. The perfume of the grass and of the flowers was heady and relaxing.

Dawlish walked with giant strides past Buckingham Palace, hardly glancing at the great, squat building. Here, the flower-beds were crammed with geraniums not yet in full bloom but already showing vivid colours.

Soon he was in Hyde Park, where hundreds of sheep were grazing and more people were lying about on the grass or in the rented deck chairs. Only when he was within sight of the new restaurant did his heart begin to beat faster. He had not the slightest idea what Jumbo would look like. It was he who would be recognised, and the other man who would have to make the approach.

It was exactly half-past three.

He went into the restaurant, which was open all day, and ordered coffee, choosing a window seat as far away as he could get from other customers. From where he sat, he had a perfect view of the park, of the sun shimmering on the Serpentine, where a hundred small boats seemed to make moving patterns on the open lake and among the shadows cast by the tall trees. Then, a man who had been sitting in another window seat beckoned a waiter, gave him a sealed envelope and indicated Dawlish. Dawlish, who had noticed this by-play, opened the envelope and took out what it contained.

It was a head and shoulders portrait of Felicity. She was either asleep—or dead.

CHAPTER SEVENTEEN

JUMBO

Very slowly, Dawlish turned the photograph over. On the back, in pencilled block capitals, was the terse instruction: *follow the man in grey.* The man in grey, in the window, was now rising. A waiter came up to Dawlish, who suddenly slapped his pocket, and said with a groan:

'I've forgotten my wallet.'

He got up and went off, the man he was expected to follow being already at the door. Dawlish felt absolutely defenceless, but the time had come to go along with these men. He had done everything he possibly could at distance; now there must be confrontation. The man in grey stopped at an old fashioned Bentley, a fairly common-place car, not especially noticeable, but big and roomy. He opened the back door and stood aside. There was a driver at the wheel, peaked cap pulled down low over his eyes.

'Where are we going?' asked Dawlish.

'To our apartment.' For the first time, Dawlish had a really good look at the man's face. He was startled out of his calm, for it was surprisingly like that of the dead Smith. The likeness was more one of expression and type rather than a similarity of feature. 'You will be quite safe,' the man assured him. 'We know when we have come to terms, Mr. Dawlish.'

Dawlish got in, the man climbed in beside him and the car started off.

'We have a number of apartments,' his companion went on. 'It is difficult to use Bell Court, now, so we are not going there.'

Dawlish nodded.

As they sat back, he looked out on the parked cars, then at the Royal Albert Hall, then along Princes Gate. Soon the car turned to the right, to blocks of mansion flats behind the circular building, coming to a standstill near a corner. They went into a tall, wide, hall, where doormen stood on duty and a lift man stood halfway along. The impression was gloomy and Victorian.

'We are going to the fifth and top floor,' the man told Dawlish.

'Are you Jumbo?' Dawlish asked.

'No. You can call *me* Mr. Smith,' the man smiled and the remark seemed part of a macabre joke. The lift was automatic and there was only just room for the two of them. When it stopped, a doorman on the fifth floor pulled open iron grill gates. Several doors led off this landing, and one of them was open. The man in grey stood aside, and Dawlish entered a long hall, which was furnished with rich mahogany pieces against a pale green carpet. Two doors led off this, and from one came a man.

Dawlish felt quite sure that this was 'Jumbo', the man he had come to see.

Tall and broad-shouldered, there was something almost regal in the finely-cut features. Immaculately dressed in a dark suit, his iron grey hair was swept back in wings from his forehead, while about his eyes, almost as blue as Dawlish's, there was a disturbing directness.

Dawlish said drily: 'Mr. Jumbo, I presume.'

'Yes, Mr. Dawlish.'

For a moment Dawlish thought that he was going to offer to shake hands, but at the last moment he seemed to change his mind, merely motioning towards the doorway.

'Please come in.'

The room, furnished with bronze-coloured chairs and couches, was curiously bare; yet it was warm enough. No one else was present, and no one else came in. The double doors closed; Dawlish wondered whether the last 'click' was a key turning in the lock.

'Do sit down.' There was another movement of the hand, betraying a touch of almost feminine elegance. 'I am assured that you were not followed, Mr. Dawlish. So you really came on your own.'

'I said that I would,' Dawlish said simply.

'Men of their word are so rare,' murmured Jumbo. It was an absurd name for him, and could hardly have been less appropriate. 'I imagine you won't want to beat about the bush.'

'I want my wife,' Dawlish said, and his heart began to hammer against his ribs. 'If you have harmed her . . .'

'No, Mr. Dawlish, she is unhurt. Drugged, but unhurt. And you can get her back very simply, by acceding to our request.

118

There are no other conditions at all.'

'Just by joining The Authority,' Dawlish remarked drily.

'We would be both pleased and proud to have you,' Jumbo declared. 'What *is* your price, Mr. Dawlish?'

'You still ask on the basis that every man has one,' murmured Dawlish.

'Of course.'

'You really could be wrong, you know.'

'I don't believe so. Now that you know more about our range of operations, you realise, of course, that we can offer you a much greater inducement than we yet have,' said Jumbo. 'Mr. Dawlish, we have come to the conclusion that The Authority needs you. You could step immediately into a high position within the hierarchy—the same level as I, indeed, and there is only one higher. You had best know that as well as five Jumbos'—he did not seem to think the name even slightly funny—'there are five Leos—a committee of five which make *all* The Authority's decisions. Those of my rank, and below, simply carry the decisions out. And ...' He paused for a long drawn out moment, and then went on: 'As we both want and need you, you may set your own price.'

When Dawlish didn't comment, he went on: 'In all of our experience we have never met a man like you, Mr. Dawlish. We have never met an individual with such strength of will, nor one who would take such risks and be so positive. I repeat —you may name your own price.'

Ten million pounds, poor Smith had advised. Ten million pounds.

'And there is an aspect which has probably not occurred to you,' went on Jumbo, in his near pontifical manner. 'We seek no political or social privileges, but we have a great deal of power. Whatever position you would like in British National affairs, we could get for you.'

'I see,' said Dawlish. 'If I had a hundred million pounds I would probably want to sit at a table and count my money.' He actually smiled. 'I've no political ambitions of any kind, I assure you.'

'Do you know, I believe you really are a man without ambition,' Jumbo said, obviously amazed.

'Oh, I've a lot of ambition,' Dawlish assured him. 'I want to see a crime-free world, for instance.'

'Do you indeed! Dawlish ...' Jumbo hesitated, as if to make

sure that he had the whole of Dawlish's attention, and then went on: 'Crime is comparative. Once, we, The Authority, are no longer under threat from existing governments we need commit no crime of any kind. We could spend a fortune on the police to help to create a crime-free state, or even a crime-free world; provided only we could make our profits—our lawful profits—without hindrance. Such things as felonies, ordinary crimes of violence, fraud, embezzlement—you would have every opportunity to stamp all of these out, Dawlish, if that is really what you want.'

'That is what I want,' Dawlish affirmed.

'Then we have the beginning of understanding. Tell me, Mr. Dawlish, what would you do if we gave you a hundred millions capital and a million pounds a year income.'

'Stamp out as much crime as possible,' Dawlish answered.

'Surely you have some personal desires.'

'Oh yes,' Dawlish agreed promptly. 'To get my wife back and live in peace with her.'

Jumbo hesitated for some seconds and then leaned forward and pressed a bell-push. As he took his hand away, he went on, as if marvelling:

'You make it sound so very simple.'

'It is simple,' Dawlish said earnestly. 'Bring her to me. Until she is with me I won't even begin to bargain.' He looked levelly at Jumbo, and did not even glance round when the door opened and a footman wheeled in a trolley. Out of the corner of his eyes he saw plates of cakes, bread and butter, and the thinnest of sandwiches. 'Now all we need is a hostess to serve. My wife is a very good hostess.'

As he spoke, the door opened and a woman entered. On that first instant Dawlish did not believe it possible, but the next moment he knew beyond all doubt that this was Felicity. He bounded to his feet, and rushed towards her. The other man pushed the trolley away just in time.

'Pat!' gasped Felicity.

He reached and seized and held her; and he could feel her heart beating furiously. He thrust her away and looked her up and down, almost greedily. Her grey-green eyes were slightly hazy, as if she were fresh from sleep or drug, but she looked a delight—outwardly she was not harmed at all. He drew her to him again and kissed her, and then whispered in her ear:

'Take your cue from me.' Aloud, he cried as if he could not

believe his eyes. 'You're all right? They didn't hurt you?'

'I'm not even really sure where I am,' Felicity told him. 'I've been asleep.' She looked at Jumbo, then back at Dawlish and asked helplessly, 'Where *am* I? What am I doing here, Pat? I was in a room on my own, a strange room. I haven't the faintest idea how I got here.'

'You were drugged and brought here,' Jumbo told her easily. 'Would you care to pour out, Mrs. Dawlish? ... I will have lemon in my tea, please.' He pushed a chair up to her, and the trolley in front of the chair. 'I want you to use your influence to make your husband see what is best for his own good and your good,' he went on: 'I represent an organisation which is prepared to pay him a fabulous sum and an almost unbelievably high income if he will only join us. And as one of us he could achieve what he obviously most desires: a victory in the war against crime. He is being very obstinate, and I hope you can persuade him to be more reasonable.'

Felicity was pouring tea quite calmly.

'He is a very obstinate man,' she observed.

'I've no doubt you are fully aware of that,' said Jumbo drily.

'And if he refuses that kind of offer he must doubt whether it's honest,' Felicity remarked. 'Don't you, Pat?'

'Yes,' Dawlish answered.

'You see,' Felicity smiled pleasantly at Jumbo. 'Nothing would persuade him, least of all, I.'

Jumbo took a cup of tea and Dawlish noticed how beautifully his hands were kept, how well-shaped the nails, how pale and unblemished the skin. He pursed his lips, sipped, pursed them again and then told her:

'He gambled with your life this morning.'

'I've no doubt,' said Felicity. 'He has before.'

'If you don't manage to persuade him, you will never get out of here alive, nor will his own life be a long one,' Jumbo said, in the lightest of voices.

'Pat,' said Felicity, 'that sounded very much like a threat. What delightful cakes!' She took one and placed it on a plate. 'I shouldn't really, but...'

For the first time, Jumbo frowned.

'You really are a most remarkable couple,' he said testily. 'But perhaps you don't fully understand the situation. You see, you don't really have a choice. Either you join us, or you die.'

'Your friend Smith II assured me that I could come here safely, and be allowed to go,' Dawlish said.

'Not everyone worships the truth as you do, Mr. Dawlish.'

'So I've discovered,' Dawlish said, drily. 'Still, we'll have a little truth. Fel, this gentleman is one of several Jumbos serving an organisation which I call Omniscience Unlimited, and they call The Authority. He and his Authority have corrupted world governments, great business houses, politicians at all levels, policemen and public servants. Nothing, and no one, is inviolate. He thinks I could control a world police force which would do exactly what it was told. How does the idea appeal to you, darling?'

'You couldn't possibly do it,' Felicity replied promptly.

'Mrs. Dawlish!' exclaimed Jumbo.

Dawlish stood up.

It was one of his most swift and baffling movements. One moment he was sitting holding a cup and saucer, the next he was on his feet, taking Jumbo's wrist. He hoisted the astounded man to his feet, and spun him round, his right arm pushed high behind his back in a hammer lock.

'Get behind the door!' he ordered Felicity. He pushed Jumbo forward, bodily. As he neared the door it opened, and two men stepped inside; obviously the room was covered by closed circuit television and people outside knew much of what was going on. One man was armed with a knife, the other a gun. But Jumbo was in front of Dawlish and there was no room for a man to push past on either side. 'Slam!' ordered Dawlish, and Felicity slammed the door with all her strength, so that it crashed into one man and sent him reeling into the other. Dawlish flung Jumbo to one side, and threw his whole weight against the door. It crushed the arm of a third, who cried out in agony. The arm disappeared. Dawlish closed the door and turned the key in the lock quite calmly and as he was doing this, Felicity pushed a heavy chair against it. She showed only a quiver of nervousness.

Jumbo was struggling to his feet.

Dawlish went across to him and the expression on his face was such that the man cringed back. Dawlish used his favourite punch, bringing his hand down on the back of the man's neck, and Jumbo collapsed.

Outside, there was a great deal of shouting, and a bell began to ring. Felicity straightened up from turning the chair over on its side so that it could not run on its castors, and turned breathlessly to Dawlish. Her eyes were clear now; glowing.

'Nice work,' he said, and gave her a hug.

'What next?' she asked, with remarkable calm.

'Fire,' said Dawlish. 'With luck the Fire Brigade will still work without permission from The Omniscient Authority.' One arm around her waist, he went to the window, taking out a cigarette lighter. 'Pity to burn these curtains,' he remarked. 'They look pretty good quality silk, don't they?' He flicked the lighter into flame, and Felicity held up a corner of the curtain. The tiny flame grew and began to run up the side of the long curtain. Once this was burning he started on the other—then, with both sides burning freely, he repeated all this at the second window.

'Lean out and shout fire!' he urged.

Felicity pushed up a window. Her first cry was stifled when smoke caught at her throat, but the second rang out clearer. Dawlish leaned out of the next window and bellowed:

'*Fire! Help! Fire!*'

One after another passers-by began to wave reassurance, and a policeman appeared, running. Dawlish stared at the window but kept an eye open on Jumbo, who had not stirred. The curtains blazed. There was banging at the door but it did not even begin to give way. In an astonishingly short time a fire-engine alarm sounded, and it swung round the crescent a few seconds afterwards. Dawlish watched with fascinated interest as the firemen ran up the escape, uncoiled the hoses, did everything with great precision.

Suddenly a man appeared at the window.

'Like to help the lady out, first, sir?' he asked.

'Gladly,' said Dawlish. 'And I'll go back for the other chap. I think he's been overcome by the fumes.'

He helped Felicity out, and the fireman steadied her; then he went back for Jumbo. If he could get the man away from here, alive, then he might be on the verge of breaking The Authority.

CHAPTER EIGHTEEN

BREAKTHROUGH

Dawlish was prepared for anything to happen as they reached the ground. For shooting in order to release or to kill Jumbo; for a tear gas attack; for a mass raid from the big mansion block. None of these things happened immediately. There was a thickening, jostling crowd, as firemen bent their hoses towards the fiery windows. Jumbo was still unconscious and a man—a doctor?—was bending over him. Felicity was looking down on the man as if she could not believe the transformation in her situation. A police sergeant came up.

'Isn't it Mr. Dawlish?'

'Yes,' Dawlish said, and gripped the man's arm in fierce urgency. 'Get an ambulance and take this man to Bow Street. Have at least two cars with you and a dozen men, he mustn't escape or be got at. *Is that clear?*' he rasped.

'Yes, sir. I . . .' the sergeant broke off, then squared his shoulders. 'I'll see to it.'

'Treat him like a radio-active victim. Keep everyone away from—that's *it!*' breathed Dawlish. 'Spread it around that he is radio-active! What hospital can cope?'

'St. George's, sir. It has a special unit, but——'

'Cancel Bow Street, take him to St. George's. *Can* you cope, sergeant?'

The sergeant had a big, square face and a determined jaw. 'I can and will, sir.'

'It's more vital than you can ever guess,' Dawlish raised his voice. 'He was exposed to radio activity, that's the trouble. He's a very sick man.'

People gaped. There were horrified murmurs, and immediately the crowd began to break up. 'Radio *active*,' a policeman echoed, and looked at several of his colleagues; to their eternal credit, none of the policemen moved away. The sergeant went up to the ambulance driver as the men kneeling by Jumbo stood up—— God! Could this be one of The Authority?

Jumbo looked perfectly all right.

'Move back,' policemen began to say.

'Pat,' said Felicity, taking his arm. 'Look over there.' She was looking towards the main entrance of the flats, and Dawlish was in time to see four men, all well-dressed stepping from the doorway towards a Rolls-Royce with a chauffeur at the door. There was an air of urgency about them and he needed no telling that they were on the run. He saw a police patrol car turn into the crescent, and suddenly ran towards it. The driver, already slowing down, stopped.

'That Rolls-Royce,' Dawlish said urgently. 'It must not get away. We want those men.'

The man beside the driver glanced round, and the driver suddenly revved his engine. Dawlish skipped to one side. The car door slammed and the chauffeur scrambled into his seat. The police car swung round in a wide arc, pulling up in front of the Rolls-Royce. Dawlish ran after the police car.

'Nice work!' he said gaspingly. 'I'm Dawlish, Deputy Assistant Commissioner, I want to speak to the Yard.'

'All yours, sir,' a man said. 'Do you want that car held? I—*look!*'

Dozens of men began to stream out of the main entrance, some running for cars, others scurrying off on foot. Every one of them carried a brief case or overnight case, and all had the same look of urgency and haste that marked the four men in the Rolls.

'Have the ends of the street blocked,' Dawlish ordered, and grabbed the radio telephone. *Information* was already at the other end of the line. 'Deputy Assistant Commissioner Dawlish here. I am behind the Albert Hall. I want all approaches blocked. No one is to get in or out—tell Traffic and send at least a dozen squad cars ... Clear it with your A.C. or—*Good.*' Dawlish rang off—and then saw the beginning of a miracle of improvised organisation. For the men in the police car had got out and were directing foot policemen to the ends of the street; cars, even taxis, were being commandeered with hardly a 'by your leave' to block the entrances.

One small car moved from the main entrance of the house, roared and raced towards a gap in the barricade. A policeman ran to stop it and was tossed to one side. The car weaved its way past several others and went through the gap. It swung into Kensington Gore and turned left at a furious speed.

Suddenly, Felicity was at Dawlish's side saying calmly: 'Jumbo is in the ambulance, Pat.'

'Ride with him,' urged Dawlish. 'You and half a dozen

others.'

'All right,' she said, but paused. 'Darling—are we near the end?'

'We could be.'

'Be—careful,' she said. 'Be as careful as you can.'

'Never more, never greater need,' Dawlish assured her. He stepped towards the ambulance with her, while the whole of the crescent was in pandemonium. Two more police cars appeared as if from nowhere, more men streamed out of the mansion flats. Practically the whole block must have been taken over. 'Fel—how is Kathy?'

'She's a lovely little thing,' answered Felicity. Her eyes glowed. 'Bless you, darling.'

He closed the door on her and the ambulance moved off. A commandeered taxi was in front, a police car close behind. The emergency arrangements were going like clockwork, a heart-warming example of how the police were geared to take emergencies in their stride. Now, Dawlish had a moment to stand back and survey the scene, and he almost laughed aloud.

At least twenty of the men from the mansion flats were hemmed in by a police cordon made of three cars—it was an improvised pound. Most of the blocked drivers took their position fairly calmly, but there were those who resisted, and in several places men could be seen grappling with the police. The ambulance alone was allowed through the gap, its bell clanging. A plain clothes policeman called to Dawlish:

'The Yard for you, sir.'

Dawlish strode to the police car and took up the telephone. Immediately the deep voice of Sir Hugh Warrender, the Commissioner, came over the air: Warrender had been out of town with Sir Arthur Kemp, the Assistant Commissioner for Crime, or Dawlish would have consulted him at the beginning of the affair.

'Dawlish—I hope you know what you're doing,' Warrender said abruptly.

'Thank you for backing me, sir. I'm sure I do.'

'What charges will you prefer against these people you are holding?'

'Attempted murder, for a start,' Dawlish answered. 'Kidnapping. I think even a treason charge might stand.'

'Hump. I certainly hope something will. I understand there are some thirty prisoners.'

'There could be many more,' Dawlish told him.

'Where do you propose to put them?' demanded Warrender. 'There's no room in any police station.'

'I'd like to put them in any building where they can be sealed off,' Dawlish said.

'Such as the Tower of London, I suppose,' Warrender said with heavy sarcasm.

'Many a true word,' Dawlish began, and then his voice sharpened: 'Two floors of the old building of Scotland Yard are empty, sir. Can we use them? The entrances can be blocked off quite easily.'

'I will arrange it,' promised Warrender, abruptly. 'When am I going to know what it's all about?'

'Give me until six or seven o'clock, will you?' Dawlish pleaded.

'If you haven't got a foolproof explanation you know that you'll be removed from your post, don't you?' said Warrender. 'And I would be too.'

'I don't think either of us need worry,' Dawlish assured him. 'There's one other thing.'

'Dawlish! You dismay me. There can't be anything else!'

'I need a squad of men to go through the whole of Victoria Mansions,' Dawlish went on stubbornly. 'It needs combing with a fine tooth comb. There's been some kind of activity there which needed a lot of men.'

'I'll see Andrew,' promised Warrender.

Fifteen minutes later, the Assistant Commissioner for Crime in person arrived with a squad of men trained in searching premises of every kind. He was a short wiry-looking man who was in no mood to argue or delay. 'We'll take your word that it's necessary, Pat. What are we looking for?'

'Records of any kind,' said Dawlish. 'And for God's sake look out for fire or a delayed action bomb.' He grinned. 'Andrew, I'm serious! We need to examine the contents of the cases which the men have brought out, too. And we need a clearing house for them. Need to get them away from here in case the place blows up.'

'Isn't the Albert Hall closed for a week?' asked Kemp.

'Ah,' said Dawlish. 'Brilliant idea! Will you fix it?'

'I don't know what's going on,' Kemp said. 'But you wouldn't stick your neck out like this unless it was necessary. All right.' He walked off.

Dawlish watched him go, and then took another look round the crescent. There were comparatively few people here now except for the police, and there were as many police as there were men from the mansions flats. The fire escape was still there and two firemen were coming out of the main entrance. The roads had all been effectively blocked, and there were barricades of cars and *Road Works* signs which could be removed to allow police and official cars to come in. Two or three onlookers avid for sensation still stood at one barricade.

Dawlish had a stirring sense of exhilaration. So far, obviously, there had been no serious infiltration by The Authority into the police, an odd failure, and another indication of their strange faith that nothing, and no one, could seriously impede them.

This particular building had obviously housed a large number of staff and important records, but there were others, such as Bell Court. The very speed and thoroughness of his onslaught had made the difference between failure and success, but——

It could not be the end.

Up to now, The Authority, so unused to opposition, hadn't put up a fight, had simply tried to escape, but—they *would* fight. Or some of them would. The question was when? He had achieved this tremendous victory simply because he had seized a chance when it had come and had taken The Authority unawares, but their enormous power was such that they must already be preparing for the counter attack.

Would this be planned by the 'Leos'?

Had only the Jumbos been here?

There was one way in which he might possibly find out: by talking to the Jumbo he knew. The man might be so shocked by what had happened that he would now talk freely, as Smith had done. Dawlish decided that he could get on with that part of it now. The danger here was past, Kemp would do as well, or better, than he. He walked across to the sergeant who had so quickly grasped the situation earlier, and said warmly:

'Thoroughly good job, sergeant.'

'*You're* a bloody marvel,' the sergeant replied, his voice resonant with feeling. 'Never seen anyone get things moving so fast. Er—could I ask what it's all about, sir?'

'Corruption in high places,' Dawlish answered. He hesitated, and then asked with a faint smile: 'Do you ever wonder what's got into this country? Whether it *is* going bad?'

'Decadent, that's my word, <u>sir</u>. Don't know what things are coming to these days.'

'What we've uncovered today could be one of the main reasons for it,' Dawlish told him. 'I can't be more explicit at the moment. Couldn't be if I wanted to,' he added with a smile. He had a word with the Fire Officer in charge and with the four policemen from the first patrol car to reach the scene, then walked towards one of the barricades. Suddenly it occurred to him that he hadn't a car. Ridiculous. And that Felicity was safe. Wonderful! And that everything he had done paled into insignificance against this. Very insignificant against this. Very satisfying, but—a forthcoming counter attack was inevitable. From what direction would it come?

He was soon back at the same spot in his reasoning: that he should see Jumbo and try to make him talk.

A Chief Inspector came up, briskly.

'You looking for transport, sir?'

'Yes,' said Dawlish. 'I had a lift here.'

'I'll gladly place a Divisional car at your disposal,' the man offered. 'Do you wish to drive yourself, or will you have a chauffeur?'

Dawlish deliberated. He liked driving himself but there were the minor difficulties of parking, and the output of concentration which he needed for solving of greater problems.

'I'll have a driver, I think,' he decided.

First, he must go to the St. George's Hospital. Next, to his own office. After that ... he couldn't make up his mind. It was not simply that he was in a mood of confusion, not even that he needed time to relax while his mind digested the astounding events of the past few hours. He got into a black Vauxhall with a driver, radio-telephone and everything else he needed, and realised that he was terribly thirsty. He needed tea more than anything else—my God, what a tea party! That trolley had been wheeled in a little before four o'clock. He glanced at his watch, and saw that it was exactly five twenty-five.

'Less than an hour and a half since I arrived,' he marvelled aloud.

He sat back, sitting cornerwise so that he could stretch out his long legs. Nearly half-past five. Rush hour. Londoners were on their way home in their millions, and hadn't the faintest idea what had been going on in their midst.

He had told the driver St. George's, and they were going along Knightsbridge, so they should be in the hospital within five minutes. He closed his eyes and moistened his lips. It wasn't unusual after a period of furious action to feel tired and thirsty. Twenty years ago he would have had a pint of beer, and been ready for another fierce encounter by now. Of course, he hadn't slept long last night, and an hour's sleep would do him no harm; even forty winks. He closed his eyes and half dozed.

Slowly, through this mood of lethargy, he began to realise that something was wrong. They were travelling too fast. Knightsbridge, with Hyde Park Corner, then the swing round past the old gates of Green Park, then the traffic snarl as one went along Grosvenor Street behind St. George's—none of these lent themselves to speeding.

He opened his eyes, and knew in a moment what was wrong. They were going along the one way road in Hyde Park towards Marble Arch. He did not shift his position, but suddenly he was very alert, his whole body keyed up for action. They passed Grosvenor House, so they were three-quarters of the way along this thoroughfare.

Where was he being taken? Bell Court?

He gave little thought to that, much more to the remarkable skill with which his abduction had been planned and carried out. The 'will you drive yourself' had fooled him, of course. The Chief Inspector at the Albert Hall, and this driver, were under The Authority. Here was another shattering instance of corruption among the police. It did not appear to have gone to the very high-ranking officers, yet, but half-a-dozen at Detective Inspector rank could do an enormous amount of harm.

He could stop the driver now. If it came to a point he could knock the man out, lean in front of him and take the wheel; it would be easy to steer into the grass verge. But what he needed to know was where they were going. It could surely only be to see a higher rank within The Authority.

In other words, to someone whose rank was Leo.

If he could find out where they worked from then he might have more than broken through: he might have won.

CHAPTER NINETEEN

LEO

Dawlish sat still and utterly silent. The car was forced to slow down as it reached the traffic near Marble Arch. Would they go along Bayswater Road, along Edgware Road or along Oxford Street? He felt sure that Bell Court had been written off, since the Prof. had been there, but perhaps he had been missed.

They turned along Bayswater Road, only minutes from Bell Court. He caught a glimpse of the towering central building of the concourse, which seemed all glass, and reflected the evening sun in pale yellows and near-whites. Now he was faced with another problem: when to reveal the fact that he knew he had been abducted. He saw the driver turn his head, obviously to look at him in the mirror, but his eyes were almost closed, he must look as if he were asleep.

The police were watching Bell Court in strength, remember.

They turned off the Bayswater Road towards Bell Court, and he no longer had any doubt where they were heading. He saw a car with a man sitting in it and knew that it was a police car. The man was in full view of the front of Bell Court—ah! There were several Yard men with a clear view, the moment he stepped out he would be recognised. His urgent task was to find a way of telling them he wasn't here of his own free will. He needed to send an SOS message. SOS or 999 would do.

The car pulled into the carriage way where the Prof. had driven the other night, and then he *saw* the Prof. There was no shadow of doubt; that renowned expert in disguise was at a manhole, only twenty yards away from the huge glass doors of Bell Court. He glanced up at the car and saw Dawlish, his berry-brown face quite free from expression. And out of the mists of the past there came to Dawlish the signs which he and the Prof., Ted Beresford and dozens of others had used whenever they could not safely speak. The 'SOS' or 'I need help' sign was very simple: a finger on the left hand rubbing the lobe of the left ear.

Dawlish had no time to make it then.

The car slowed down, and the driver said: 'Here we are,

sir.' A doorman opened the car door and his solid body blocked the doorway. He had a small automatic pistol in his hand, and he spoke so that only Dawlish could hear.

'This has a silencer. Get out.'

Dawlish, pretending to be taken utterly by surprise, lowered his head and started to get out.

'Don't raise any alarm, or I'll shoot you in the guts,' the doorman said, huskily.

Dawlish got out, stood up, glanced back and glimpsed the Prof. out of the corner of his eye, and while pretending to hitch his collar up, made the finger to ear gesture. He had no doubt that the Prof. saw, nor that he would understand. Two men stood close by.

'You won't get away from here alive if you try anything,' the doorman threatened.

'What the hell is all this?' Dawlish began. 'I'm supposed to be——'

'Inside.' The doorman gave him a push, and Dawlish, pretending to be more affected than he was, staggered in. Four other men were in the big foyer as well as a woman who stood by one of the three lift doors. She gave Dawlish a scared look. A bell clanged and a lift stopped, bright arrow pointing upwards. A solid phalanx of men were behind Dawlish, even with his phenomenal strength he had no chance of breaking through.

Three men entered the lift with him, each holding a small automatic. One pressed the top button; so they were going up to the penthouse, in fact the nineteenth floor. There was no name beneath the letters PH. The lift went up silently; Dawlish did not realise how fast until it stopped, making his stomach heave. The doors slid open.

Three men stood at the entrance, covering him; the other three followed him out, and now he was in the middle of a group of six.

This was a wide luxurious passage. There was a thick purple carpet underfoot, and hanging tapestries of rare beauty. Wall lights suitable for a palace. To the right and left were doors, and one of these stood ajar, with two men in front of it. They were in ordinary suits, but no one could have doubted that they were guards.

All this time, Dawlish had not made a single gesture of resistance.

He did not speak as, so closely guarded that he could hardly turn about, he was taken into the apartment and through a wide, double doorway. This led to a large, beautifully appointed room, which was unoccupied. It might have been a room in a palace. More double doors led off in one direction and as Dawlish entered, these opened slowly, as if by remote control.

Inside were five men.

They were placed like a panel of judges, two each side of a central figure who sat in a higher, throne-like chair which gave him a more impressive, more regal air, than the others. They all stared at Dawlish while the guards filed into the room, a beautiful chamber of gold colours and vari-coloured mosaics lit by soft lighting from the walls. Dawlish knew that all six of his guards were covering him with their guns. He stood in the centre of the room, like a supplicant; or a man on trial. For a few moments there was silence, and this gave him a chance to study all five of the faces before him. The men were of similar height, their ages in the middle forties, but there was no way of being sure, for undoubtedly each was disguised. It was not that they were made to resemble each other, nor that they were made to look like other, specific men. The disguise, cleverly if theatrically done, was simply to conceal their real appearance. Whoever they were, not one of them was likely to be recognised. Each had make-up. Each had sufficient eye-shade on for his eyes to look very bright. Each had an 'air' almost of arrogance, certainly of distinction. They were dressed alike in dark grey suits which were slightly Edwardian in style.

Dawlish wished there was a chair for him.

His head was throbbing, and sometime in the rush near the Albert Hall, he had banged his left knee; it was aching, twitching. So was the knife scratch at his wrist. But nothing would have made him speak first, or show any signs of fatigue.

He did not know how long he stood there. A minute could seem an age at such a time of tension. He judged that three or four minutes had passed, at least, before the man in the middle spoke. He had a pleasantly modulated voice, and enunciated the words clearly through hardly moving lips.

'There is just one chance for you, Mr. Dawlish,' he said. 'One chance, and very little time.'

Dawlish paused, as if deliberating, before he asked: 'A

chance for what?'

'To save your life. To save what you believe in. And to save your wife.'

'Ah,' said Dawlish. 'Interesting.' He smiled, mechanically. 'I do assure you that I can think just as well sitting down as standing up. Even people being tried on a charge of murder are allowed that much leniency. And—ah—any kind of drink would be welcome, from tea to beer.'

The man in the middle raised his left hand, and someone behind Dawlish moved. Dawlish felt something touch the back of his legs, and a man spoke almost into his ear:

'You can sit.'

He lowered himself, finding the padded leather arms and the padded seat of a chair. He crossed his legs and sat upright. There was a great relief all over his body; until this moment he had not realised how utterly exhausted he was. But he had to respond soon.

'Thank you.' He paused a moment. 'And in order to save my wife's life and my own, what do I have to do?'

'Join us,' the speaker answered.

'Join The Authority Omniscient?'

'You doubtless used the word Omniscient in jest, but it serves very well. We *are* virtually omniscient. We have a comprehensive survey of the political, social, industrial and commercial resources and military commitments and requirements of every nation and every company which has substantial capital. We really can direct the affairs of the world, Dawlish, but we do need you, or someone like you, particularly at this transitory stage.'

'I thought I'd already done too much damage,' Dawlish said.

'You are wrong. The damage done is not irreparable, but it could become so very soon. Let me remind you again: there is very little time. A matter of hours, only. All the documents which were taken from Victoria Mansions this afternoon were in code. We have duplicates, of course, their loss in itself is not of significance, but if they were decoded and their true nature as well as the nature and extent of our activities were discovered, then the danger would be lethal. You see, I am taking a leaf out of your own book, with'—he glanced at the men on either side of him, and continued—'with the full understanding and agreement of my colleagues.'

'You mean,' said Dawlish, as if he could not believe his ears, 'you are not a dictator?'

'I mean just that. I am the Chairman of the controlling body of The Authority, that is all. We make all of our decisions together and before we carry them out we have complete unanimity. you should realise that by now we really have infiltrated everywhere, even into the Metropolitan Police Force although not yet in any great numbers. Now, Mr. Dawlish, we want the men you have arrested and charged released. We want you to do these things in such a way as not to incriminate yourself, except so far as we are concerned. We shall of course have absolute proof of your part in it, proof we can use against you at any time. Once this is done you will be for ever subject to the rules of The Authority. It can be a very pleasant and, indeed, luxurious life. You will not only be far better off than you are now, but you will have much greater power. Moreover, you will—as you have already been told—be able to do much towards stamping out crime in the sense that society understands it today. A good society cannot afford to permit indiscriminate robbery, crimes of violence, sex crimes, all the crimes of the calendar. If you have the modern methods —which would be provided—and enough men, and if you are ruthless enough, and your judges are also ruthless, you should be able to stamp out crime in little over a year. Moreover, as other big cities saw your success, they would—with The Authority's help—reduce their own incidence of crime. You could indeed be the leader of police forces throughout the world. There is no other way in which you could possibly achieve all of these things.'

He stopped, with an air of finality. Soon it was obvious that they were all waiting for Dawlish to respond. A man appeared at Dawlish's side, with a bottle of lager and a glass already half filled, he wondered fleetingly whether this could be poisoned, or drugged, and decided that there would be little purpose in that; they wanted his help and they must surely want him sober. He drank the lager. It was like nectar.

'All I have to do is to be ruthless,' he remarked.

'Better than being a sentimentalist,' the man in the middle said shrewdly, 'and, in the end, far less distinctive.'

'I see,' said Dawlish, and finished the lager. 'That was good. Thank you.'

'Mr. Dawlish,' the man went on. 'Time is already slipping away. I have told you how little there is. Are you ready to make your decision now?'

Very slowly, Dawlish said: 'I shall need a little time.'

The spokesman for the group looked suddenly pleased, and there was relaxation on the faces of the others. He thought: they think I'm beginning to see it their way. He wondered how soon the Prof. would report to Childs, and what action the police would take. There was no certainty that he would be able to save his own life but at least he could be ready to take the slightest chance.

'You may have half-an-hour,' the spokesman conceded. 'No more,' and he smiled a curious, supercilious smile which put a shaft of fear into Dawlish. 'And you must spend it constructively, Mr. Dawlish, not in vain hope. You believe, no doubt, that your friend Ledbetter, known as the Professor, has told the police you need help. I do assure you that he hasn't.'

Ledbetter? The Prof. The shaft of fear grew deeper, and must have shown itself on Dawlish's expression, for the spokesman remarked:

'I see you are perturbed.' He raised his left hand again and almost at once a man appeared from behind Dawlish, small, with a lined berry-brown face and merry eyes, and very lively movements. For the first time since he had come in here, Dawlish felt the weight of utter hopelessness; not fear or dread, but hopelessness. His whole world seemed to grow dark.

'Ledbetter,' ordered the spokesman. 'Disillusion Mr. Dawlish.'

The Prof. turned to Dawlish, and there seemed something strange about his smile, although he sounded perky enough.

'Sorry about this, Major, but you wasn't to know I'm the make-up expert for The Authority. You know I've always been pretty good but you never knew how good. Got a team of experts working under me, too, it would never do to let anyone know what any of these gentlemen really looked like, would it? Take a tip from me, Major. I was as honest as the day was long for years. Honest as the day, but never had two tanners to rub together. Honest—hungry and honest, that was me. I got tired of it. This job pays well, and if I have to lie a bit, okay, I lie. Put up a pretty good show the other night, didn't I? And even today, when you saw me you thought it was just a matter of time, didn't you? Well—you're through, Mr. Dawlish. You've met your match.' He stopped at last, and the room was very quiet. The Prof. looked straight at Dawlish

for a few moments and then turned his head, unable to face
the expression in Dawlish's eyes. After a long pause, he turned
to the five men.

'That all for now, Mr. Leo?'

'You may go,' said the spokesman.

There was no sound as the Prof. went out. Dawlish could
not restrain himself from looking round. The six men were
still grouped in the half circle, and a man was opening the
door for the Prof. It closed behind him without a sound.

The spokesman said almost feelingly: 'You may have your
half-an-hour for reverie now, Dawlish. There is an ante-room
on the right where you may be on your own. But you have no
longer time than that. Either you will agree, or you will be
thrown from this window to your death. It will, of course, be
taken as suicide. And as our true selves, very eminent and
respectable men, we shall make it clear that you came to us
with an infamous proposition. We shall offer proof, quite
easily manufactured, that *you* were in fact a member of The
Authority, and when faced with disclosure, preferred to kill
yourself rather than face your wife and friends when the truth
was revealed.'

The spokesman stopped.

A door opened to Dawlish's right, and the guards closed in
on him and led him towards the ante-room. This was quite
large and pleasantly but not ostentatiously furnished. There
was one big window, half-shuttered now. The door closed behind Dawlish, with hardly a sound. He went across the room,
drawn as by a magnet to the window. It was in the same wall
as the main room windows and he peered out and down,
seeing the same marble surface below, the same inevitability of
death.

The only way he could possibly avoid it was by saying 'Yes'.

CHAPTER TWENTY

A NEST OF TRAITORS

Dawlish stood by the window, face set, teeth gritting. Perhaps a dozen people were in sight, moving about the concourse of Bell Court; quite a number of them were walking their dogs, one elderly man being dragged along by a Great Dane which threatened to pull him toppling. At a high-rise building, perhaps half-a-mile away, a group of workmen crawled up and down a scaffolding. To his right Dawlish could see the great red buses, roaring down Edgware Road: to his left was the traffic along Bayswater Road and Hyde Park.

London looked so normal, the grass and trees so green. He must have stood there for five minutes. He had twenty-five—*twenty-two or three* minutes.

He thought, sick at heart, of the Prof. If such a man as Ledbetter couldn't be trusted, who could? For a few moments he felt furiously, bitterly angry about the Prof.'s defection. But it was no use losing his head, no use losing self control. The Authority had infiltrated everywhere. If there was a hope of any kind, he had to find it in the next twenty-five-*twenty-two or three* minutes.

He did not think he had a chance. He had bull-dozed his way through to the present situation, and sooner or later his 'luck' had to end. He had pushed it too far. And if he had to jump—well, God knew he had had a good run. A wonderful run. If he could spend a few minutes with Felicity—no! He rejected the very thought. It would fill her with despair. Worse, it would mean she would die with him. Looking back, if he had a regret it was that they had not been able to have children. Nothing any specialist had been able to do had made the slightest difference. He saw a mental picture of Kathy Kemball's face against the sky. It would be a strange twist of fate if Felicity cared for the child when he ...

What the hell was the matter with him? There was time, there was life, there was hope! Hope out there in London, in the world.

Something dropped slowly past the window.

At first glimpse he thought it was a bird, but as his eyes

focused on it, he realised what it was, and for an instant was astonished. Was he seeing another illusion, like the child's face? Was he—*no!* He was seeing something he could hardly believe, a tiny floating parachute with a 'man' dangling at the end of it. It was exactly like the one he had found on the back of Kathy's door. It reached the wide ledge of the window, and the legs and body of the parachutist crumpled up. The parachute fell slowly, as real ones did, and fluttered towards the edge. If it went over it would drag the doll with it. He pushed suddenly at the window, half-expecting it to be locked—but it opened wide enough for him to get his arm through.

The parachute stayed on the ledge.

Dawlish took the toy soldier, handling it as if it were of flesh and blood, then just managed to get his head out of the window and looked upwards, but he could see nothing except jutting ledges and guttering. His heart was thumping, he closed the window and drew back into the room.

Then he saw a tiny label on the parachutist's back saying: '*Unscrew the head.*' He hesitated only for a second, his fingers feeling big and clumsy. The toy was no larger than his middle finger. He took the head firmly and twisted anti-clockwise. Almost at once the head began to move. At last it was in his hand. Inside the hollow body was a roll of paper, and he shook this out on to his palm, put the toy down and unrolled the paper. His heart had never beat so fast.

He read: '*Whatever you do, protect yourself as well as you can. The place is surrounded, and detachments of the military, with some police units, will move in at five o'clock precisely. I am on the roof, which has been under surveillance all day. So has the window of the room you are in. It might be possible for you to force the window and climb up but my strong advice is for you to barricade the door of the room you are in.*'

The note was signed: *Jim Childs.*

If he went back into the other big room then the first thing they would do when the raid started was to shoot him. Something screamed out in him to be there, to see what happened when the raid began; but it would be folly. The raid was due at the moment he was due back before the Council of Leos.

Odd, vivid thoughts flashed into his mind. How had Childs known where he was? God! *He hadn't been sure he could trust Childs.* How had the raid been organised? *That didn't matter, it had been.* Was there any way into this room except by the door? *He could seek one but there was hardly time to search.* He went to the door and tried the handle, not surprised to find it locked. It opened inwards, however, he could barricade it. He made a quick survey of the room, selected a huge couch with its back against the wall and bent his back to it, moving it without making any noise. He up-ended it, then brought chairs and a heavy marble-topped table to strengthen the barricade. Next he pulled up the heavy carpet, Indian hand woven and very heavy, so that when they pushed against the door they would push against the carpet.

There was nothing left to do but wait.

He glanced at his watch; there were only ten minutes to go. He picked up the toy parachutist, and wondered where Childs had got it, how it had been dropped, whether it had been used as a message bearer before...

Perhaps it had always been meant to carry messages!

He went to the window again. This time, he saw jeeps and small trucks in the side streets, saw three companies of infantry on 'manoeuvres' in Hyde Park, then became aware of many more helicopters in the vicinity than usual; two of them flew very close. If there was to be a raid it might come from the air as well as from the ground.

He stood watching, fascinated.

Quite suddenly, real parachutists began to drop down from helicopters and the concourse suddenly became alive with soldiers, picking themselves up and shrugging themselves free of their harness. Most disappeared towards the side and main entrances, and as the last one vanished he heard banging at the door of his room.

He spun round.

The door was under terrific onslaught but it was holding. He could do nothing to help—he, Dawlish, the man of action. He could hear running footsteps above the banging, shouting and then a barked command: 'Every man stand still!'

For a moment there was silence; the banging and the footsteps stopped. Next moment there was a crack of a shot, followed by a sharp:

'I told every man to stand still.'

After a pause, one man, he thought the spokesman Leo, said in a strained, incredulous voice: 'So he defeated us.' There was only a moment before Childs spoke, in his slow but positive way.

'You might as well have given up when you knew Dawlish was involved.' He gave a dry little laugh. Then, in a louder voice: 'Are you there, Mr. Dawlish?'

'I'm not only here,' called Dawlish, beginning to take the barricade down, 'but my ears are burning.' A young subaltern was now able to push the door open an inch or two, then squeeze through. 'I'll take over, sir.' He pulled the door wider, and Dawlish stepped out on to the landing.

Childs, several officers and half-a-dozen young soldiers were there. So were the five Leos and the guards. As he watched them, Dawlish wondered fleetingly what was passing through their minds. And he wondered who they were, knowing that it would not be long before they were unmasked.

Childs came towards him.

'*How?*' asked Dawlish, almost helplessly.

'If you'll come with me to the office, sir, I can best show you,' said Childs. 'The raid near the Albert Hall gave us the key, of course, and some of the documents found there were quickly decoded.' He ignored the five Leos, and Dawlish gave them only a glance. They went down in the lift, and out to a foyer completely taken over by the military, as was the fore-court and the concourse. A few plain clothes policemen were also there. In a car driven by one of Dawlish's staff, Childs went on:

'Every government office, every big business, all the major boards of the nationalised industries—everywhere had been infiltrated. But not the Army, and there appears to have been comparatively little infiltration in the police forces.'

Dawlish muttered: 'Small mercies.'

'A few other things,' Childs went on. 'The Authority is world wide, and for its strong-arm men uses people from one country in another. This was how the passport affair began. And there is a lot of evidence that The Authority has for years got exactly what it wanted by waiting for the right moment to get the right man.'

'I see,' Dawlish said. 'I see.'

The car started off: 'This was all evident in the first search among the papers at the Albert Hall,' Childs went on. 'And of course you have been closely watched by us—you were trailed by helicopter, among other things. That was how we were able to act so quickly at the Albert Hall. We knew where you were.

I thought it better you didn't know what precautions *I* was taking.'

Dawlish said gruffly: 'Didn't trust me, eh?'

'I certainly didn't trust you not to bite off more than you could chew,' admitted Childs. He fell silent and they said nothing as they drove along Whitehall, then to the old New Scotland Yard.

In the office were Felicity and Ted Beresford, and Beresford was smiling and Felicity's eyes were glowing and very, very bright. Childs slipped in past Dawlish, and this was obviously the cue for Felicity to say:

'We really owe it to Kathy, Pat. I gave her the parachute and she unscrewed the head of the soldier—she said her father often sent her play messages that way. But there was a lot more than play messages in the one you found.'

She paused, and Childs took up the story.

'There was a load of microfilm, sir. The film gave the names of some of the leading men in The Authority—and it named Bell Court as the main headquarters. The Right Honourable Montgomery Bell is *very* highly placed in the organisation. David Kemball knew much more than we realised. In fact he was on to the whole business, sir. He tried to blackmail The Authority, as far as I can find out. He did the same as you, sir, started out on the passport clue and went on from there. But it took him several months, whereas it took you a day or two!'

'Always the fast worker,' Beresford said deep-voiced. 'Well, I must be off. Don't worry about Kathy, Fel. Joan will look after her until you've decided what to do.'

He went out, happily.

'You don't want me any more, do you?' Childs asked.

Dawlish looked at him long and steadily.

'I don't think I'll ever be able to do without you, Jim. And I know I will never keep anything from you again.' He put out his hand, which Childs instantly gripped in his own.

It would take months to clear up this mess, of course, months to restore the confidence needed. There were major decisions of policy to be made by the Government whether to disclose what had happened or to clean up all departments quietly. Dawlish was all for publicity and open trials, but his wasn't the decision and he did not complain. Back in his flat he allowed a pleasant tiredness to sweep over him. It was good to be with Felicity, good to hear her moving about as he took a leisurely bath, put on an old sweater and a pair of slacks, then crossed to the window. Felicity came from the kitchen, her hands white with flour. He pulled her to him nearly squeezing the breath out of her body.

'I'm hungry,' he announced.

'I expect you are,' said Felicity. 'Steak, chips, fried onions, pancakes, cheese and biscuits, in about twenty minutes. Can you hold out that long?'

'Needs must if the devil drives. May I help?'

'If we're going to eat in the kitchen you can lay the table and open some beer and ...' They were still chatting as they went into the kitchen, and then suddenly Dawlish changed the subject and the mood.

'Fel—what about Kathy?'

Felicity turned from the grill to look at him.

'What do you mean?'

'I had the funniest thought while I was waiting for doom to overtake me: that you wouldn't be alone if you had Kathy.' When she didn't answer at once, he went on: 'I took to the child. So did you. And she took to us. Am I crazy?'

'No, darling,' Felicity said, slowly. 'Not particularly. Not about that, anyhow.' She was pushing the onions round the pan, the steam rising about her face, misting her expression. 'But she's been on her own so much. Too much. With Joan and Ted she'd be with the other children, and lead a much more normal life.'

Felicity turned, empty handed, and went on almost pleadingly: 'She couldn't, with us, could she? It isn't that I don't want to help her, I *would* love to have her, I do need——' She broke off. 'Pat, I'm thinking about the child.'

Dawlish said slowly and very quietly: 'I know. I think you're probably right. If Ted and Joan are serious——'

'I'm absolutely sure they are,' Felicity assured him.

They stared at each other for a few seconds and then she turned to take the steaks from under the grill.

Next day, when Dawlish saw the child, she rushed to him as if to an old friend; but within minutes, she was back with the Beresford children, playing.

A SELECTION OF FINE READING
AVAILABLE IN CORGI BOOKS

War

☐ 552 09055 7	SIDESHOW	*Gerald Bell* 30p
☐ 552 09161 8	INSTRUMENTS OF DEATH	*W. A. Harbinson* 40p
☐ 552 08874 9	SS GENERAL	*Sven Hassel* 35p
☐ 552 08779 3	ASSIGNMENT GESTAPO	*Sven Hassel* 35p
☐ 552 09144 8	THE STRAITS OF MESSINA	*Johannes Steinhoff* 40p
☐ 552 08986 9	DUEL OF EAGLES (illustrated)	*Peter Townsend* 50p
☐ 552 08936 2	JOHNNY GOT HIS GUN	*Dalton Trumbo* 30p
☐ 552 09004 2	THE LONG WATCH	*Alan White* 25p
☐ 552 09092 1	WEREWOLF	*Charles Whiting* 35p

General

☐ 552 09100 6	FANNY HILL'S COOKBOOK	*L. H. Braun & W. Adams* 40p
☐ 552 09169 3	THE FASCINATING FORTIES	*Barbara Cartland* 30p
☐ 552 08926 5	S IS FOR SEX	*Robert Chartham* 50p
☐ 552 09151 0	THE DRAGON AND THE PHOENIX	*Eric Chou* 50p
☐ 552 98958 4	THE ISLAND RACE Vol. 1	*Winston S. Churchill* 125p
☐ 552 98959 5	THE ISLAND RACE Vol. 2	*Winston S. Churchill* 125p
☐ 552 09168 5	FIVE PATIENTS	*Michael Crichton* 40p

Western

☐ 552 09147 2	IN THE DAYS OF VICTORIO (illustrated)	*Eve Ball* 40p
☐ 552 09095 6	APACHE	*Will Levington Comfort* 30p
☐ 552 09170 7	SUDDEN—DEAD OR ALIVE	*Frederick H. Christian* 30p
☐ 552 09113 8	TWO MILES TO THE BORDER No. 70	*J. T. Edson* 25p
☐ 552 08280 5	RETURN TO BACKSIGHT No. 53	*J. T. Edson* 25p
☐ 552 08282 1	APACHE RAMPAGE No. 55	*J. T. Edson* 25p
☐ 552 09058 1	RIDE THE DARK TRAIL	*Louis L'Amour* 25p
☐ 552 09112 X	THE DAYBREAKERS	*Louis L'Amour* 25p
☐ 552 09165 0	THE GALLOWS EXPRESS No. 19	*Louis Masterson* 25p
☐ 552 09098 0	PAINTED PONIES	*Alan Le May* 35p
☐ 552 09097 2	VALLEY OF THE SHADOW	*Charles Marquis Warren* 35p

Crime

☐ 552 09162 6	A NEST OF TRAITORS	*John Creasey* 30p
☐ 552 09163 4	ROGUES RAMPANT	*John Creasey* 30p
☐ 552 09164 2	THERE GOES DEATH	*John Creasey* 30p
☐ 552 08640 1	RED FILE FOR CALLAN	*James Mitchell* 30p
☐ 552 09073 5	INNOCENT BYSTANDERS	*James Munro* 30p
☐ 552 09111 1	THE ERECTION SET	*Mickey Spillane* 40p
☐ 552 09056 5	SHAFT	*Ernest Tidyman* 30p
☐ 552 09072 7	SHAFT'S BIG SCORE	*Ernest Tidyman* 30p

*All these books are available at your bookshop or newsagent: or can be ordered direct from
the publisher. Just tick the titles you want and fill in the form below.*

CORGI BOOKS, Cash Sales Department, P.O. Box 11, Falmouth, Cornwall.
Please send cheque or postal order. No currency, and allow 6p per book to cover the
cost of postage and packing in the U.K. and overseas.

NAME ....

ADDRESS ....

(March 73) ....